Princess
Treasury

This is a Parragon Book

This edition published in 2005

Parragon

Queen Street House

4 Queen Street

Bath BA1 1HE, UK

Design and project management by Aztec Design

Illustrated by

Chameleon Designs, Daniel Howarth, Paula Martyr, Anna Leplar,

Claire Mumford, Chris Forsey, Diana Catchpole, Robin Edmonds and Jo Brown.

Cover Illustration by John Dillow

ISBN 1-40545-742-2

Printed in China

Princess
Treasury

p

Contents

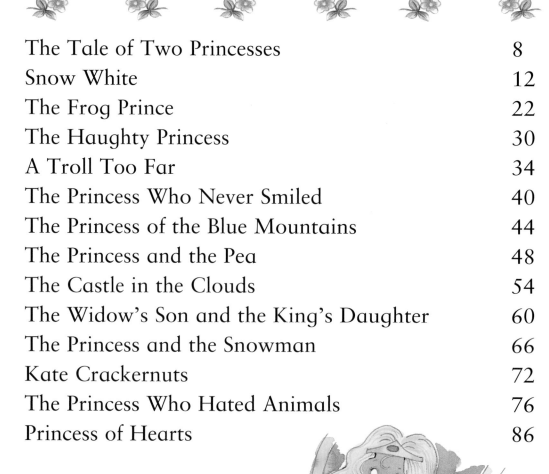

The Tale of Two Princesses

Long ago there were twin princesses called Charmina and Charlotte. Even though they were twins, the princesses were very different. In fact they were opposites. Princess Charmina was gracious and charming to everyone. She curtsied politely to the king and queen. And she stood quite still while the royal dressmakers came to fit her new ball gown.

Princess Charlotte was very different!

"Why do I have to dress like a puffball?" grumbled Princess Charlotte when it was her turn to have a new ball gown fitted.

"How dare you speak to us like that!" her parents cried.

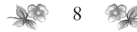

But she did dare. She dared to run barefoot through the gardens until her hair looked like a bush. She dared to wear her shabbiest clothes. In fact, she didn't behave like a princess at all!

One day there was to be a ball at the palace. The guests of honour were two princes from the next kingdom. The two princesses, dressed in their new ball gowns, kept getting in the way of the preparations. "Why don't you go for a walk until our guests arrive?" suggested the queen. "But stay together, don't get dirty and don't be late!"

The two princesses walked to the bottom of the palace gardens.

"Let's go into the forest," said Princess Charlotte to her sister.

"I don't think we should," said Princess Charmina. "Our gowns will get dirty." But Princess Charlotte had already set off.

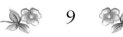

"Wait for me!" called Princess Charmina. "We must stay together!" They wandered deeper and deeper into the forest. They crunched through fallen leaves, listening to the birds singing.

"I think we should go back," Princess Charmina told her sister. "We'll be late for the ball."

Just then they heard a strange noise.

"Let's turn back!" said Princess Charmina, afraid.

"It may be someone in distress!" said Princess Charlotte.

"We must go and help!"

Although Princess Charmina was scared, she agreed. "But we must get back in time for the ball."

"Don't worry, we will," said Princess Charlotte.

They set off again, going even deeper into the forest. Finally, they came upon two horses in a clearing, but there was no sign of their riders. Just then they heard voices calling out, "Who's there?"

At first, the two princesses couldn't see where the voices were coming from. In the middle of the clearing there was a large pit – an old bear trap. They peered over the edge. Princess Charmina clapped her hand over her mouth in astonishment. Princess Charlotte burst out laughing. There at the bottom of the pit were two princes.

"How do you do?" said the first prince.

"Well, don't just stand there," said the second prince. "Help us out!"

The two princesses found ropes and threw one end down to the princes. They tied the other end to their horses. Soon the princes were rescued and laughed with the princesses. They all set off to the palace together.

On their return they found everyone in the palace in a state of panic. The king and queen were angry when their daughters returned late looking so dirty. But their anger turned to joy when the two princes explained what had happened.

Everyone enjoyed the ball. The two princesses danced all night with the two princes. And, do you know, from that time on, Charlotte paid more attention to her gowns and hair. And Charmina became a little more playful and daring than before!

Snow White

*L*ong, long ago, in a faraway land, there lived a king and queen who had a beautiful baby girl. Her lips were as red as cherries, her hair as black as coal and her skin as white as snow – her name was Snow White.

Sadly, the queen died and years later the king married again. The new queen was very beautiful, but also evil, cruel and vain. She had a magic mirror, and every day she looked into it and asked, "Mirror, mirror on the wall, who is the fairest one of all?"

And every day, the mirror replied, "You, O Queen, are the fairest!"

Time passed, and every year Snow White grew more beautiful by the hour. The queen became increasingly jealous of her stepdaughter.

One day, the magic mirror gave the queen a different answer to her question. "Snow White is the fairest one of all!" it replied.

The queen was furious. She ordered her huntsman to take Snow White deep into the forest and kill her.

But the huntsman couldn't bear to harm Snow White. "Run away!" he told her. "Run away and never come back, or the queen will kill us both!" Snow White fled deep into the forest.

As Snow White rushed through the trees she came upon a tiny cottage. She knocked at the door and then went in – the house was empty. There she found a tiny table with seven tiny chairs. Upstairs there were seven little beds. Exhausted, she lay down across them and fell asleep.

Many hours later, Snow White woke to see seven little faces peering at her. The dwarfs, who worked in a diamond mine, had returned home and wanted to know who the pretty young girl was.

Snow White told them her story and why she had to run away. They all sat round and listened to her tale.

When she had finished, the eldest dwarf said, "If you will look after our house for us, we will keep you safe. But please don't let anyone into the cottage while we are at work!"

The next morning, when the wicked queen asked the mirror her usual question, she was horrified when it answered, "The fairest is Snow White, gentle and good. She lives in a cottage, deep in the wood!"

The queen turned green with rage; she had been tricked. She magically disguised herself as an old pedlar and set off into the wood to seek out Snow White and kill the girl herself.

That afternoon, Snow White heard a tap-tapping at the window. She looked out and saw an old woman with a basket full of bright ribbons and laces.

"Pretty things for sale," cackled the old woman.

Snow White remembered the dwarfs' warning. But the ribbons and laces were so lovely, and the woman seemed so harmless, that she let her in.

"Try this new lace in your dress, my dear," said the old woman. Snow White was thrilled and let the lady thread the laces. But she pulled them so tight that Snow White fainted.

Certain that at last she had killed her stepdaughter, the queen raced through the forest, back to her castle, laughing evilly.

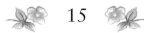

That evening, the dwarfs returned home. They were shocked to discover Snow White lying on the floor – lifeless. They loosened the laces on her dress so she could breathe and made her promise once again not to let any strangers in when they were at work.

The next day, when the mirror told the queen that Snow White was still alive, she was livid and vowed to kill her once and for all. She disguised herself and went back to the cottage.

This time the old woman took with her a basket of lovely red apples. She had poisoned the biggest, reddest one of all. She knocked on the door and called out, "Juicy red apples for sale."

The apples looked so delicious that Snow White just had to buy one. She opened the door and let the old woman in.

"Oh my, what pretty, rosy cheeks you have, deary," said the woman, "the very colour of my apples. Here, take a bite and see how good they are." She handed Snow White the biggest one…

Snow White took a large bite and fell to the floor – dead. The old woman fled into the forest, happy at last.

This time, the dwarfs could not bring Snow White back to life.

Overcome with grief, they placed her gently in a glass coffin and carried it to a quiet clearing in the forest. And there they sat, keeping watch over their beloved Snow White.

One day, a handsome young prince came riding through the forest and saw the beautiful young girl in the glass coffin. He fell in love with her at once and begged the dwarfs to let him take her back to his castle.

At first the dwarfs refused, but when they saw how much the prince loved their Snow White, they agreed.

As the prince lifted the coffin to carry it away, he stumbled, and the piece of poisoned apple fell from Snow White's mouth, where it had been lodged all this time. Snow White's eyes fluttered open, and she looked up and saw the handsome young man.

"Where am I?" she asked him in a bewildered voice. "Who are you?"

"I am your prince," he said. "And you are safe with me now. Please will you marry me and come to live in my castle?" He leant forward and kissed her cheek.

"Oh, yes, sweet prince," cried Snow White. "Of course I will."

The next day, the magic mirror told the wicked queen of Snow White's good fortune. She flew into a rage and disappeared in a flash of lightning.

Snow White married her prince, and went to live in his castle. The seven dwarfs visited them often, and Snow White and her prince lived happily ever after.

The Frog Prince

There was once a king who had but one daughter. Being his only child, she wanted for nothing. She had a nursery full of toys, a pony to ride and a wardrobe bursting with pretty dresses. But, for all this, the princess was lonely. "How I wish I had someone to play with," she sighed.

The princess's favourite toy was a beautiful golden ball. Every day she would play with her ball in the palace garden. When she threw the ball up in the air, it seemed to take off of its own accord and touch the clouds before landing in the princess's hands again.

One windy day the princess was playing in the garden as usual. She threw her golden ball high into the air, but instead of returning to her hands, the wind blew the ball into the fishpond. The princess ran to the pond, but to her dismay the ball had sunk right to the bottom. "Whatever shall I do?" wailed the girl. "Now I have lost my favourite toy." And she sat down beside the pond and cried.

All at once she heard a loud PLOP! and a large green frog landed on the grass beside her. "Eeeuugh! Go away, you nasty thing!" screamed the princess.

To her astonishment, the frog spoke to her. "I heard you crying," he said in a gentle voice,

"and I wondered what the matter was. Can I help you in any way?"

"Why, yes!" exclaimed the princess, once she had got over the shock of being addressed by a frog. "My ball has sunk to the bottom of the pond. Would you fish it out for me?"

"Of course I will," replied the frog. "But in return, what will you give me if I do?"

"You can have my jewels, my finest clothes and even my crown if you will find my ball," said the princess hastily, for she was truly eager to get her favourite toy back.

"I do not want your jewels, your clothes or your crown," replied the frog. "I would like to be your friend. I want to return with you to the palace and eat from your golden plate and sip from your golden cup. At night I want to sleep on a cushion made of silk next to your bed and I want you to kiss me goodnight before I go to sleep, too."

"I promise all you ask," said the girl, "if only you will find my golden ball."

"Remember what you have promised," said the frog, as he dived deep into the pond. At last he surfaced again with the ball and threw it onto the grass beside the princess. She was so overjoyed she forgot all about thanking the frog – let alone her promise – and ran all the way back to the palace.

That evening the king, the queen and the princess were having dinner in the great hall of the palace, when a courtier approached the king and said, "Your majesty, there is a frog at the door who says the princess has promised to share her
dinner with him."

"Is this true?" demanded the king, turning to the princess and looking rather angry.

"Yes, it is," said the princess in a small voice. And she told her father the whole story.

"When a promise is made it must be kept, my girl," said the king. "You must ask the frog to dine with you."

Presently, the frog hopped into the great hall and round to where the princess was sitting. With a great leap he was up on the table beside her. She stifled a scream.

"You promised to let me eat from your golden plate," said the frog, tucking into the princess's food. The princess felt quite sick and pushed the plate away from her. Then to her horror the frog dipped his long tongue into her golden cup and drank every drop. "It's what you promised," he reminded her.

When he had finished, the frog stretched his long, green limbs, yawned and said, "Now I feel quite sleepy. Please take me to your room."

"Do I have to?" the princess pleaded with her father.

"Yes, you do," said the king sternly. "The frog helped you when you were in need and you made him a promise."

So the princess carried the frog to her bedroom, but as they reached the door she said, "My bedroom's very warm. I'm sure you'd be more comfortable out here where it's cool."

But as she opened the bedroom door, the frog leapt from her hand and landed on her bed.

"You promised that I could sleep on a silk cushion next to your bed," said the frog.

"Yes, yes, of course," said the princess, looking with horror at the froggy footprints on her clean, white sheets.

She called to her maid to bring a cushion.

The frog jumped onto the cushion and looked as though he was going to sleep.

"Good," thought the princess, "he's forgotten about my final promise."

But just as she was about to get into bed, he opened his eyes and said, "What about my goodnight kiss?"

"Oh, woe is me," thought the princess as she closed her eyes and pursed her lips towards the frog's cold and clammy face and kissed him.

"Open your eyes," said a voice that didn't sound a bit like the frog's. She opened her eyes and there, standing before her, was a prince. The princess stood there in dumbstruck amazement.

"Thank you," said the prince.

"You have broken a spell cast upon me by a wicked witch. She turned me into a frog and said the spell would only be broken if a princess would eat with me, sleep beside me and kiss me."

They ran to tell the king what had happened. He was delighted and said, "You may live in the palace from now on, for my daughter needs a friend." And indeed, the prince and princess became the best of friends and she was never lonely again. He taught her to play football with the golden ball and she taught him to ride her pony. One day, many years later, they were married and had lots of children. And, do you know, their children were particularly good at leapfrog.

The Haughty Princess

There was once a king who had a very beautiful daughter and many dukes, earls, princes, and even kings came to ask for her hand in marriage. But the princess was proud and haughty and would have none of them. She would find fault with each suitor, and send him off with a rude remark.

And so it went on, until every unmarried duke, earl, prince, and even king, had been rejected, and her father thought she would never find a man she liked.

Then a prince arrived who was so handsome and polite that she found it hard to find fault with him. But the princess's pride won, and she looked at the curling hairs under his chin and said, a little reluctantly, "I shall not marry you, Whiskers."

The poor king finally lost his temper, "I'm sick of your rudeness. I shall give you to the first beggar who calls at our door for alms, and good riddance to you!"

Soon a poor beggar knocked at the door. His clothes were in tatters, his hair dirty, and his beard long and straggling. Sure enough, the king married his daughter to the bearded beggar. She cried and tried to run away, but there was nothing for it. The beggar led his bride into a wood. He told her that the wood and the land around it belonged to the king she had called Whiskers. The princess was even sadder that she had rejected the handsome king, and hung her head in shame when she saw the poor, tumbledown shack where the beggar lived. The place was dirty and untidy, and no fire burned in the grate. The princess put on a plain dress and helped her husband make the fire, clean the place and prepare a meal.

The beggar gathered some twigs of willow, and after their meal, the two sat together making baskets. But the twigs bruised the princess's fingers, and she cried out with the pain.

The beggar was not a cruel man, and so he gave her some cloth and thread, and set her to sewing. But although the princess tried hard, the needle made her fingers bleed, and again tears came to her eyes. So the beggar bought a basket of cheap earthenware pots and sent her to market to sell them.

The princess did well at market on the first day, and made a profit. But the next morning, a drunken huntsman rode through the market place, and his mount kicked its way through all the princess's pots. She went home in tears.

The beggar spoke to the cook at the palace of King Whiskers, and persuaded her to give his wife a job as a kitchen maid. The princess worked hard, and the cook gave her leftovers to take home for her husband. The princess liked the cook, and got on quite well in the kitchen, but she was still sorry she had rejected King Whiskers.

A while later, the palace suddenly got busier. King Whiskers was getting married. "Who is going to marry the king?" asked the princess. But no one knew who the bride was going to be. The princess and the cook decided to go and see what was going on in the great hall; they hoped to catch a glimpse of the mysterious bride. They opened the door quietly and peeped in.

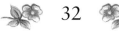

King Whiskers was in the room, and strode over when he saw the door open. "Spying on the king? You must pay for your nosiness by dancing a jig with me." The king took her hand, led her into the room, and the musicians played. But as they danced, puddings and portions of meat began to fly out of her pockets, and everyone in the room roared with laughter. The princess began to run to the door, but the king caught her and took her to one side.

"Do you not realise who I am?" he asked her, smiling kindly. "I am King Whiskers, and the beggar, and the drunken huntsman who broke your pots in the market place. Your father knew who I was, and we arranged all this to rid you of your pride."

The princess was very confused. All sorts of emotions welled up inside her, but the strongest of all these feelings was love for her husband, King Whiskers.

The palace maids helped her to put on a fine dress fit for a queen. She went back to her husband, and none of the guests realised that the new queen was the poor kitchen maid who had danced a jig with the king.

A Troll Too Far

Once upon a time, in a faraway fairytale kingdom, there lived a king with a problem – a very big, very nasty problem indeed.

Now, the king lived in a proper fairytale castle, with towers and turrets, ballrooms and battlements, a wide, deep moat and a drawbridge. And underneath that drawbridge lived and lurked a very large, very smelly, very HUNGRY troll! Now trolls, as you may or may not know,

Beware of the TROLL

will as a rule eat anything, and this troll was no exception. He guzzled the goldfish that swam in the moat; he snacked on stray sheep that grazed at the water's edge (sheep are incredibly stupid!); and worse still, he stretched out one long slimy arm and snatched anything – or anyone – that ventured across the drawbridge, and gobbled it down in a gulp! Whether jousters or jesters, witches or wenches, paupers or princes, this terrible troll would gorge on them all. And as if all this were not bad enough, this left the poor king and his courtiers with yet another problem –

35

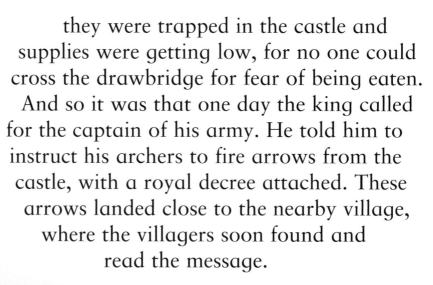

they were trapped in the castle and supplies were getting low, for no one could cross the drawbridge for fear of being eaten. And so it was that one day the king called for the captain of his army. He told him to instruct his archers to fire arrows from the castle, with a royal decree attached. These arrows landed close to the nearby village, where the villagers soon found and read the message.

The village buzzed with the news that the king was offering to grant anything within his power to whoever could rid him of the terrible troll. From the village, the news spread throughout the land and further still; and soon noblemen, knights and princes were arriving from far and near to take up the challenge and claim their reward. The greedy troll was delighted. Never had he enjoyed such a feast of fine fare, as he munched his way through each brave (or foolish) challenger.

The king was in despair. Could no one save them from their castle prison? Then, just as he had almost given up hope, a lumbering shape came looming through the mist.

"I will rid you of this terrible troll," boomed a deep and dreadful voice. As the mist cleared the king saw to his horror that the voice belonged to an even larger, even uglier, even smellier troll! But what could the king do? He was certainly not about to argue!

And so the new troll leapt into the moat and a fearsome fight took place. The two trolls thrashed and splashed, bit and scratched, pulled and tugged, roared and gnashed their teeth. They sent tidal waves crashing around the moat, and shook the castle to its foundations!

Finally, after three days and nights of monstrous struggling, the old troll was forced to accept defeat, and he stomped away into the distance, cursing and shaking his fist.

"And now for my reward!" smirked the new troll, with a gleam in his eye, slowly licking his lips. The king shuddered, and clasped the princesses tightly to him. Anything but his precious daughters!

"What is your request?" stuttered the king. "I will grant you anything in my power, as I promised."

"I'd like a new home," drawled the troll. "Beneath the drawbridge..."

"Open wide," called young Princess Grace. From beneath the drawbridge, the hideous head of the revolting new troll appeared, mouth open wide to reveal a rotting row of yellow teeth.

"Yum, yum, breakfast!" slobbered the troll. The princess leant over the drawbridge and poured a vast basket of cakes and cabbages into the troll's quivering, dribbling, open mouth.

For yes, he was huge, he was smelly, he was hideous. But he was also vegetarian – and the king was delighted!

The Princess Who Never Smiled

A long time ago, in a far-off land, a princess was born. The king and queen called her Princess Columbine. They thought she was the most precious child ever to be born. And, to make sure that she was watched over every minute of every day, they hired a nurse to look after her.

One day, the queen came to the nursery and found the nurse asleep and the little princess crying. The queen was very cross and called for the king. He told off the nurse for not watching the baby. But what the king and queen didn't know was that the nurse was really a wicked enchantress. The nurse was so angry at being told off that she cast a spell over the little baby princess:

40

"Princess Columbine will never smile again until she learns my real name!"

The king and queen were devastated. From that day on, the princess never smiled! Names were collected from all over the land. They tried all the usual names, such as Jane, Catherine, Amanda. They tried more unusual names, such as Araminta, Tallulah, Leanora. They even tried quite outlandish names such as Dorominty, Truditta, Charlottamina. But none broke the spell.

Princess Columbine grew up to be a sweet and beautiful girl. Everybody loved her. But her face was always so sad, it made the king and queen unhappy. They tried everything to make her smile. They bought her a puppy. They even hired a court jester who told the silliest jokes you've ever heard.

"Why did the pecans cross the road?" asked the jolly jester. The princess shrugged.

"Because they were nuts!" the jester laughed.

"Why did the ice cream?" the jester tried again. The princess just gazed politely.

"Because the jelly wobbled!"

One day an artist called Rudolpho came to the palace and asked the king if he could paint the princess's portrait. The king agreed on one condition. He had to paint the princess smiling. Rudolpho set up his easel beneath a large mirror and began straight away. The princess sat opposite, watching him paint in the mirror behind him. As he worked, Rudolpho asked the princess about all the people in the palace. He had soon painted the princess's portrait, all except for her smile. But he couldn't make the princess smile.

Rudolpho tried some funny drawings. He drew silly pictures of the king and queen. The princess looked on politely. Then he drew a picture of her old nurse and gave her a moustache, and underneath he wrote NURSE.

Princess Columbine gazed in the mirror. There, below the picture, was the word NURSE spelt out back to front – ƎƧЯUN.

"ESRUN," Princess Columbine said quietly. And then she smiled. "Her name is ESRUN!" laughed Princess Columbine. At last the spell was broken! The king and queen heard her laughter and came rushing to see what was happening. They were so happy that soon everyone in the palace was laughing too.

The Princess of the Blue Mountains

There was a poor widow with one son called Will. He was all she had in the world so he always had his way, and he became lazy. In the end she said to him, "Son, you must make your own way in the world. Then you will know what it is to find your own work and earn your own living." So young Will went off to seek his fortune.

Will travelled until he came to a river, which he had to cross. Seeing the rapid current and the sharp rocks he was afraid to go into the water, but a lady on the opposite bank saw him and waved at him to cross which, finally, he did.

When Will got to the other side, the lady said she would

give him food and drink if he would go into her garden and find the most beautiful flower. But Will, struck by the lady's beauty, said, "You are the fairest flower in all the garden."

Charmed by Will, the lady turned to him. "Would you be my husband?" she asked. "There will be many dangers, but I will help you." It did not take Will long to say, "Yes, I will be your husband, whatever dangers I must face."

The lady explained her story. She was the Princess of the Kingdom of the Blue Mountains. She had been stolen by a demon called Grimaldin who would do battle with Will. The lady gave Will three black sticks, one for each legion of demons, and a pot of ointment, in case he should be injured. "Use these things well, for now I must leave you."

The lady left and three legions of demons appeared. They beat Will with fearsome clubs, but the young man stopped their blows, and used the lady's sticks to beat them. Soon they were gone.

The lady returned, and was pleased to see Will hale and hearty. "Never has any man fought off the demons with such skill and courage. Tonight, twice as many demons will challenge you, so I will give you six sticks." And the lady left, giving Will a larger pot of ointment, in case he was wounded.

Sure enough, six legions of demons arrived to do battle with Will and he beat them off successfully.

The following morning the lady was delighted but said, "I must give you twelve sticks, for twelve legions will come tonight. Look out for Grimaldin, for he will come too." She left more ointment, for no one had survived a fight with Grimaldin without being sorely wounded.

Grimaldin and his twelve legions arrived, and the chief demon asked Will: "What is your business?"

"To rescue the Princess of the Blue Mountains."

"Then you shall die."

The demons attacked, and Will beat them off with the sticks, but this time Grimaldin attacked, and struck Will to the ground. The young man quickly applied the ointment and was amazed to feel well again. This time, he beat off the chief demon, who went away, howling.

The princess reappeared looking relieved. "Your greatest danger is over," she said to Will. "Take this book about the history of my family; let no one distract you from reading it. If you know all that is in this book, you will be one of my father's favourites, and he will allow you to marry me."

Will started the book. Voices tried to distract him, but he kept his eyes glued to the pages. He heard a woman selling apples and he looked up from the book. He was thrown against the apple woman's basket with such force that he passed out.

When Will awoke there was an old man sitting nearby and Will asked if he knew how to get to the Kingdom of the Blue Mountains. The man did not know, so he asked the fishes, and no fish knew the whereabouts of the kingdom. The old man said, "I have a brother who can talk to the birds of the air. He will know, or will find out from the birds."

The old man's aged brother called all the birds but none knew until the last bird, a great eagle, arrived. "I can take you to the kingdom," said the eagle. "Climb onto my back."

They landed by a house hung with black drapes. The people told Will that their master was to be fed to a giant who ate a human every day. Whoever could kill the giant would please the king, and gain the hand of his daughter in marriage.

Will knew what he must do. He put on his armour, and strode out to challenge the giant. They fought long and hard, and Will was finally the winner. The princess recognised him and when the king learned that he had killed the giant, he gave his permission for Will and the princess to marry.

After the wedding, Will's mother came to live with them at the royal castle, and they lived happily together.

The Princess and the Pea

Once upon a time, there was a prince whose one and only wish was to marry a princess – but only a true princess. In order to find her, he travelled all over the land. He met young princesses and old ones, beautiful princesses and plain ones, rich princesses and poor ones, but there was always something that was not quite right with each of them.

The prince began to despair. He called together his courtiers and announced, "I have failed to find my dream princess. We will go home to our palace without delay."

The Princess and the Pea

One dark night, there was the most tremendous storm. Lightning flashed across the sky and thunder buffeted the thick palace walls.

The prince and his parents were talking in the drawing room, when they heard a tiny tap-tapping at the window. The prince opened it, and standing there before him was a very beautiful, but very wet, young lady. Her hair was dripping, her dress was soaked through, and she was shivering.

"I am a princess," she told the prince, "and I am lost. Please may I come in and shelter from the storm?"

The prince asked the girl into the palace. He turned to the queen and whispered, "Oh, Mother, she is enchanting! But how can I be sure she really is a princess?"

"Leave it to me," said his mother, and she hurried off to have a bedroom prepared for the pretty girl.

First, the queen placed a little green pea on the mattress.

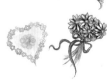

Then she ordered the servants to bring twenty thick mattresses, and twenty feather quilts, which they piled on top of the pea. The princess needed a very tall ladder to climb into bed that night!

The next morning, at breakfast, the queen asked the princess if she had slept well.

"I had an awful night!" said the princess. "I don't know what it was, but there was a hard lump under my bed, and it kept me awake all night. I'm covered with bruises!"

"At last!" the queen exclaimed. "We have found a true princess for our son. Only a real princess would have skin so tender that she could feel a pea through twenty mattresses and twenty feather quilts!"

The prince was overjoyed, and he and the princess were soon married.

As for the little green pea, after the wedding it was put on display in the royal museum – where it can still be seen today!

The Castle in the Clouds

There was once a family that lived in a little house in a village at the bottom of a mountain. At the top of the mountain was a great, grey castle made of granite. The castle was always shrouded in clouds, so it was known as the castle in the clouds. From the village you could only just see the outline of its high walls and turrets. No one in the village ever went near the castle, for it looked such a gloomy and forbidding place.

Now in this family there were seven children. One by one they went out into the world to seek their fortune, and at last it was the youngest child's turn. His name was Sam. His only possession was a pet cat named Jess, and she was an excellent rat-catcher. Sam was most upset at the thought of leaving Jess behind when he went off to find work, but then he had an idea.

"I'll offer Jess's services at the castle in the clouds. They're bound to need a good ratter, and I'm sure I can find work there, too," he thought.

His parents were dismayed to discover that Sam intended to seek work at the castle, but try as they might they could not change his mind. So Sam set off for the castle with Jess at his side. Soon the road started to wind up the mountainside through thick pine forests. It grew cold and misty. Rounding a bend they suddenly found themselves up against a massive, grey stone wall. They followed the curve of the wall until they came to the castle door.

Sam went up to the door and banged on it. The sound echoed spookily. "Who goes there?" said a voice.

Looking up, Sam saw that a window high in the wall had been thrown open and a face was eyeing him suspiciously.

55

"I... I... I wondered if you'd be interested in employing my cat as a rat-catcher," began Sam.

The window slammed shut, but a moment later a hand beckoned him through the partly-open castle door. Stepping inside, Sam and Jess found themselves face to face with an old man. "Rat-catcher, did you say?" said the old man, raising one eyebrow. "Very well, but she'd better do a good job or my master will punish us all!"

Sam sent Jess off to prove her worth. In the meantime Sam asked the old man, who was the castle guard, if there might be any work for him, too.

"You can help out in the kitchens. It's hard work, mind!" the guard said.

Sam was soon at work in the kitchens – and what hard work it was! He spent all day peeling vegetables, cleaning pans and scrubbing the floor. By midnight he was exhausted.

He was about to find a patch of straw to make his bed, when he noticed Jess wasn't around. He set off in search of her. Down dark passages he went, up winding staircases, looking in every corner and behind every door, but there was no sign of her. By now he was hopelessly lost and was wondering how he would ever find his way back to the kitchens, when he caught sight of Jess's green eyes shining like lanterns at the top of a rickety spiral staircase. "Here, Jess!" called Sam softly. But Jess stayed just where she was.

When he reached her, he found that she was sitting outside a door and seemed to be listening to something on the other side. Sam put his ear to the door. He could hear the sound of sobbing. He knocked gently at the door.

"Who is it?" said a girl's voice.

"I'm Sam, the kitchen boy. What's the matter? Can I come in?" said Sam.

"If only you could," sobbed the voice. "I'm Princess Rose. When my father died my uncle locked me in here so that he could take over the castle. Now I fear I shall never escape!"

Sam pushed and pushed at the door, but to no avail. "Don't worry," he said, "I'll get you out of there."

Sam knew exactly what to do, for when he had been talking to the guard, he had spotted a pair of keys hanging on a nail in the rafters high above the old man's head. He had wondered at the time why anyone should put keys out of the reach of any human hand. Now he thought he knew – but first he had to get the keys himself!

Sam and Jess finally made their way back to where the keys were, only to find the guard was fast asleep in his chair right underneath them! Quick as a flash, Jess leapt up onto the shelf behind his head. From there, she climbed higher and higher until she reached the rafters. She took the keys in her jaws and carried them gingerly down. But as she jumped from the shelf again, she knocked over a jug and sent it crashing to the floor. The guard woke with a start.

"Who goes there?" he growled. He just caught sight of the tip of Jess's tail as she made a dash for the door.

Sam and Jess retraced their steps with the guard in hot pursuit. "You go a different way," hissed Sam, running up the stairs to Rose's door, while the old man disappeared off after Jess. Sam put one of the keys in the lock. It fitted! He turned the key and opened the door. There stood the loveliest girl he had ever seen. The princess ran towards him, as he cried, "Quick! There's not a moment to lose."

He grabbed her hand and led her out of the tower.

"Give me the keys," she said. She led him down to the castle cellars. At last they came to a tiny door. The princess put a second key in the lock and the door opened. Inside was a small cupboard, and inside that was a golden casket filled with precious jewels. "My own casket – stolen by my uncle," cried Rose.

Grabbing the casket the pair ran to the stables and saddled a horse. Suddenly Jess appeared with the guard still chasing her. With a mighty leap Jess landed on the back of the horse behind the princess and Sam. "Off we go!" cried Sam.

And that was the last that any of them saw of the castle in the clouds. Sam married the princess and they all lived happily ever after.

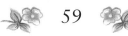

The Widow's Son and the King's Daughter

The father of a young lad called Jack died, leaving Jack and his mother penniless, so Jack had to go to work. He knew that he was no use at home, so he set off one day to seek his fortune.

After travelling far on the first day, Jack came to a house near a wood. The people of the house offered him food and a bed for the night, and the man of the house asked Jack if he needed work. Jack replied that he did. "I have a herd of cattle that needs minding," said the man. "But do not go into the field with the fruit trees. A giant lives in that field and he will surely gobble you up if you go there. He may even carry off my cattle to eat."

Jack went to the field to mind the cattle, and he had not been there long when he started to admire the fruit on the trees in the neighbouring field. There were red apples and ripe pears, as well as other fruit that Jack did not recognise.

No one seemed to be about, so Jack thought he would risk a dash into the giant's field for some fruit.

As Jack picked some of the fruit, an old woman passed along the lane by the edge of the field. She was admiring the fruit, and asked Jack to pick some for her. Looking around him to make sure the giant was not coming, Jack agreed, and soon they both had some fine, succulent fruit to eat.

"I will give you something useful in return for your favour," the old woman said to Jack. "Here are three stout rods and a sword. Whoever you stab with this sword, they will fall down dead. You need never fear your enemies."

Jack thanked the old woman, for he had been worried about the giant, and wondered whether it would stride over the hedge into his field and take his revenge for the stolen fruit.

It was not long before the giant appeared and Jack hastily climbed a tree. He had not tried the sword and wondered whether it would work. This did not put off the giant, who stepped towards the tree, held out his hand, and heaved. He tore the tree up by the roots, and as Jack fell to the ground, Jack's sword grazed his flesh. The giant fell down dead.

Jack was guarding his master's cattle the next day, when another giant appeared. "You dared to slay my brother?" the beast bellowed. Jack drew his sword and felled him with one blow. As he looked at the massive corpse, Jack wondered if there were any more in the giant's family.

On the third day, another giant appeared. Jack hid in the hollow of a tree, and heard the creature saying he must eat one of Jack's beasts. "Ask me first," shouted Jack from inside the hollow tree.

"Was it you who killed my two brothers?" roared the giant. "I shall take my revenge." But as the giant drew near the tree, Jack leapt out and stabbed him. The last of the giants was dead.

When he had got his breath back, Jack decided to go to the giants' castle to see what riches might be hidden there.

When he arrived, he told the giant's steward that he had conquered the giants and, amazed at Jack's strength, he gave the lad the keys to the castle treasuries. Jack took some of the money, then travelled back home.

Jack's country was in turmoil when he arrived. People told him that a fire-breathing monster had arrived and had demanded one young boy or girl to eat every day. Tomorrow, it was the turn of the king's daughter.

Jack found some armour, took his faithful sword and went to see the king's daughter. He told her that he had come to save her, and asked if she would marry him if he was successful. She agreed, and Jack fell at her feet. He was soon asleep with his head in the princess's lap and the princess wove a good-luck charm of white stones in his hair.

Suddenly, the monster crashed into the room. Jack woke up and immediately drew his sword. He aimed many blows at the monster, but he could not wound the beast because of the fire that came spurting from the creature's mouth.

They carried on like this for some time, Jack waving his sword and the beast spitting fire, until the monster began to tire, and slunk away.

The next day, the beast returned. The same thing happened and once again the monster grew tired and this time flapped its wings and flew away.

On the third day, Jack made a camel drink several barrels of water. When the dragon appeared, Jack made the camel spit out its water to put out the fire. Then Jack went in for the kill, stabbing the beast and cutting off its head. The princess, and all her people, were saved.

Jack and the princess were betrothed, and Jack went away for some more adventures.

After nine months, the princess had a baby, but no one knew who was the father. The king was angry with his daughter, but they went to see a fairy, who might give them the answer. The fairy placed a lemon in the child's hand and said, "Only the child's father will be able to remove this fruit."

The king then called all the men in his kingdom to the palace and each one tried to take away the lemon. But no matter how hard they tried, the fruit would not come away from the baby's hand. Finally, Jack appeared, and as soon as he touched the baby, the lemon came away.

The king was angry with Jack and his daughter, and wanted them to leave the palace. He put them in rags, set them in a rotten boat and cast them out to sea. The couple thought that their boat was about to sink, when a lady appeared. "I was the fairy who gave Jack his sword, and protected the princess from the breath of the beast," she said. "I will help you."

She repaired the boat and gave them fine robes; and so they returned to the palace.

Jack explained to the king who he was. "I saved your daughter from the monster," said Jack, producing the king's gold cup and the head of the monster. Then the princess showed him the ringlet of stones in Jack's hair. Convinced of the truth, the king allowed the couple to marry. They lived in great happiness, and eventually, Jack became king.

The Princess and the Snowman

One morning Princess Bella looked out of her bedroom window and saw that the palace was covered in a thick layer of snow. Snow lay on the turrets and along the tops of the walls. There was snow in the well and snow on the guards' hats. The palace garden was so deep with snow it looked as though it was covered in delicious icing. The snow looked fresh, inviting and untouched – apart from a line of paw prints made by Bella's pet cat, Beau.

The princess clapped her hands with glee. "I'm going to make a snowman," she cried, and rushed off to find her warmest coat and gloves. Soon she was busy in the garden rolling a great ball of snow for the snowman's body and another one for his head.

At last the snowman was finished, and she put an old hat on his head and a scarf around his neck.

"Now," thought Princess Bella, "he needs a face."

Turning to Beau she said, "Go and find the snowman a nose."

"Miaow!" said Beau and trotted off. Bella found three lumps of coal and stuck them in a row on the snowman's head to make a mouth. Then she stuck a stone on each side of his head for ears. Beau came back with a piece of carrot in her mouth.

"Well done, Beau," said Bella. "That's perfect for a nose." And she stuck the carrot in place.

At that moment there was a call from a palace window. "Bella, Bella! Come inside at once. It's time for your lessons," called the queen. Bella ran indoors and, do you know, she forgot all about giving the snowman a pair of eyes.

"I wonder when the princess will come and give me my eyes," thought the snowman wistfully. "I'd better keep my wits about me."

He listened hard with his stone ears and sniffed with his carrot nose, but there was no one there.

Night came and all the lights in the palace went out. In the middle of the night, a storm blew up. The windows of the palace rattled, the trees creaked and groaned and the wind moaned. The snowman strained his stone ears even harder and now he could hear a fearsome icy jangle and a piercing, shrieking laugh. It was the Ice Queen. As she blew past the snowman, he felt the Ice Queen's cold breath on his snowy cheek and the touch of her icicle fingers on his snowy brow. The snowman shivered with fear.

Now he heard the Ice Queen's icy tap, tap on the palace door and her howl as she slipped through the keyhole.

There was silence, then suddenly the snowman heard a window being flung open and the Ice Queen's cruel laugh.

"She's leaving," thought the snowman with relief. But what was this? Now he could hear the sound of a girl sobbing, and as the Ice Queen passed, he heard Princess

Bella's voice calling, "Help me!"

Then there was silence again, save for the sound of the wind in the trees.

"She's carried off the princess," thought the snowman. "There's only one thing to do!" He drew his breath and with all his might he shouted through his coal lips, "Help!"

He thought to himself, "No one will hear my shouts above the noise of the wind."

But soon he felt a warm glow on his cheek. "Can I help?" said a soft, kindly voice. "I am the South Wind and I can see you're in trouble."

The snowman could hardly believe his stone ears. "Oh, yes, please help," he cried. "The Ice Queen has carried off Princess Bella and I'm afraid she may die of cold."

"I'll see what I can do," said the South Wind gently, and she started to blow a warm wind. She blew and she blew and soon the Ice Queen's icy arms began to melt. Then Bella was able to slip from her cold grasp.

"It was the snowman who saved you," whispered the South Wind in Bella's ear as she carried her back to the palace.

Bella could hear the drip, drip sound of snow being melted by the South Wind's warm breath. As she reached the palace gate, the sun was rising and the snow in the garden was turning to slush. "I must see my snowman before he is gone," she thought.

There he was on the lawn. His hat was starting to slide off his head and his mouth was all crooked. She rushed over to him and to her astonishment he spoke.

"Please give me my eyes before I melt completely," he begged.

"Yes, of course I will," Bella replied. Quickly she fixed two pieces of coal in place on his melting face.

"You are so lovely," said the snowman, looking at her with his coal eyes. "I have one last request before I'm gone. Will you marry me?"

"Why, I will!" said Bella without thinking twice – for how could she refuse the request of the one who had saved her from the Ice Queen?

Bella could not bear to think that the snowman was melting away. She glanced down so that he would not see that she was crying.

"Bella," he said. She looked up and there standing before her was a prince. For once in her life she was speechless.

"Long ago, the Ice Queen carried me away – just like she did you. She cast a spell on me that meant I could only return to earth as falling snow. But by agreeing to marry me you have broken the spell," said the prince.

And so Bella and the prince were married, and lived happily ever after.

Kate Crackernuts

Long ago there lived a king and a queen. Each had a daughter: the king's daughter, Kate, was fairer than the queen's daughter, and the queen was jealous of her. The queen plotted a way to spoil Kate's beauty.

The queen visited a witch, who told her to stop Kate from eating and to send the girl to her. The queen sent Kate to the witch to ask for some eggs, but Kate had a bite to eat before she left the house.

When Kate arrived, the witch told her to lift the lid off a pot. But nothing happened. "Tell your mother to keep the larder locked," said the witch.

The next morning Kate went to the witch. On her way she saw some people picking peas. Kate had some peas to eat, so once more nothing happened when the witch asked Kate to open the pot.

The next day the queen went with Kate. When Kate lifted the lid of the pot, the head of a sheep changed places with Kate's own head. The queen was satisfied.

The queen's daughter was sorry for Kate. She covered Kate's head with a cloth and they set out to see if anyone could cure her. The two girls went far until the queen's daughter did not feel well, so they tried to find lodgings at a castle which belonged to a king.

Once the guards let them inside the castle courtyard, the girls told the people they were travellers far away from home and asked if they could have lodgings for the night. They were soon granted their wish, as long as Kate stayed up at night to look after the king's sick son. Kate was promised a purse of silver, and she agreed.

At midnight the castle clock struck twelve and the prince climbed out of bed. He put on his clothes, opened the door of his room, and went downstairs to the stables. Kate followed, making sure that she wasn't seen even when she jumped silently up on the horse behind him.

As they rode through a forest Kate picked nuts from the trees.

When they reached a green hill, the prince stopped his horse. "Open and let the prince enter," said the king's son.

"And his lady too," said Kate, quietly.

An opening appeared and they rode in.

Kate saw a fine hall, filled with dancing lords and ladies.

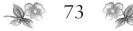

She watched as fairies and a child played with a wand. "Three strokes of the wand will make Kate's stepsister well," said a fairy. So Kate rolled nuts across the floor to the child until he forgot the wand, and Kate hid it in her apron.

When a cock crowed, the prince mounted his horse, and with Kate behind him, they rode back to the castle.

As soon as she could, Kate tapped her sister three times with the wand, and she was better. Then Kate's sister touched Kate with the wand, the sheep's head disappeared and Kate's fair face returned. Kate then sat by the fire, cracking nuts and eating them as if nothing had happened.

When the king asked her how his son had been, she replied that he had had a good night. The king asked her to sit with him one night more, and he offered her a purse of gold pieces in payment if she would agree.

So the next night Kate sat by the prince's bedside once more. When the clock struck midnight, the prince went to his horse and rode again to the green hill, as before.

The king asked Kate to watch his son for one night more. "How shall I reward you this time?" asked the king.

"If I look after him again tonight, let me marry your son," she replied.

KATE CRACKERNUTS

As on the two previous nights, the prince went to his horse at midnight and rode to the green hill. Kate sat quietly as the prince danced. Once more, she noticed the small child who had had the wand. This time, he was playing with a bird, and Kate heard one of the fairies say, "Three bites of that bird would cure the prince."

So Kate rolled nuts across the floor to the child until he had forgotten the bird, and Kate hid it in her apron.

They returned to the castle, and instead of cracking her nuts as before, Kate plucked the bird and roasted it. When he smelt the bird, the prince said, "That smells very fine. I would like to have some of that meat to eat." Kate gave him one bite, and the prince rose up, supporting his weight on his elbow; she gave him a second bite, and he sat up in bed; she gave him a third bite and he got up, and sat by the fire.

When the king and the others came into the room they found the prince and Kate cracking nuts and eating them together. The prince looked as well as could be, and soon they were married. Meanwhile, the king's other son married the queen's daughter. They all lived in happiness, and were never again troubled by royal jealousy.

The Princess Who Hated Animals

When she was just a little girl, Princess Kalimena was bitten by one of her father's hunting dogs. Then she was scratched by the palace cat and one morning, while she was waiting for the groom to fix her saddle in place, her horse stepped on her foot and bruised it badly.

After that, Kalimena was scared of animals and, as she grew, so her dislike of them grew until it was a fully grown hatred. If something had fur, feathers, claws, whiskers, fins or a tail, she hated it and would not allow it near her.

So when Princess Kalimena became Queen Kalimena, the first thing she did was to pass a very unpopular new law.

"From this day forth, all animals are banned from the land," she declared.

Now this was not such a difficult thing to do in the palace grounds. The horses were removed from their stables, and the dogs were taken out of their cosy kennels.

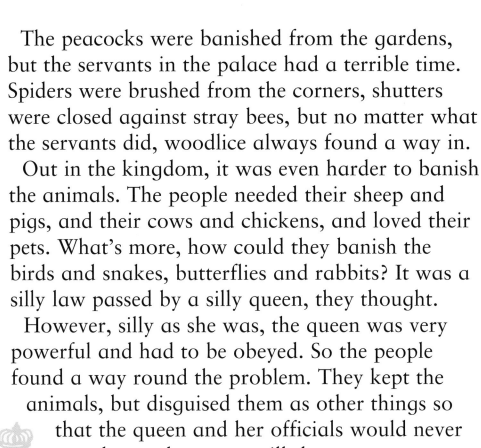

The peacocks were banished from the gardens, but the servants in the palace had a terrible time. Spiders were brushed from the corners, shutters were closed against stray bees, but no matter what the servants did, woodlice always found a way in.

Out in the kingdom, it was even harder to banish the animals. The people needed their sheep and pigs, and their cows and chickens, and loved their pets. What's more, how could they banish the birds and snakes, butterflies and rabbits? It was a silly law passed by a silly queen, they thought.

However, silly as she was, the queen was very powerful and had to be obeyed. So the people found a way round the problem. They kept the animals, but disguised them as other things so that the queen and her officials would never know they were still there.

One day, Queen Kalimena decided to take a tour of her land. She rumbled along the country lanes in her carriage, pulled very slowly by four very hot and tired guards.

"Can't you go any faster?" she yelled.

The queen waved to her subjects as they worked in the fields and she was pleased to see that there were no animals. However, some of the people did look very strange. Their clothes didn't fit them at all well and they didn't seem to be doing very much work. And once, when she was passing a hairy-looking scarecrow, she was convinced she heard it bleat like a goat.

When she became hungry, the queen stopped at the nearest house to have lunch. On this particular day, the house they stopped at belonged to Tasha and her family.

"The queen is coming," warned her father as he rushed into the house. "Are the animals hidden?"

"Yes," replied Tasha. "Just throw the tablecloth over the pig and we'll be ready. Now, stand very still," she said to the rabbits on the shelves, who were pretending to be bookends. "And you two," she said to the cranes in the corner, "you're supposed to be lamps, remember, so no squawking."

The queen strode in haughtily.

"Your Majesty," said Tasha's mother, curtsying. "How lovely to see you."

"Oh, what a gorgeous shawl," said the queen, looking at two white swans that Tasha's father had hung on a peg with strict instructions not to flap their wings. The queen picked up the swans and draped them over her shoulders. "Oh, it fits me beautifully," she said. "So warm and surprisingly heavy." And then the queen sat down.

Now the chair that the queen sat in was really a kangaroo with a cloth thrown over him and when she sat down he did his best not to gasp or fidget.

Tasha's mother put a wonderful display of food on the table (which was actually the pig), and the queen started to eat and drink.

Tasha, her mother and father watched nervously. Suddenly there was a bleating cry from outside, and a thump. One of the sheep, which the farmers had put into the trees to make them look like low-lying clouds, had fallen to the ground.

"What was that?" said the queen, looking up from her meal.

"Oh, just the baby," said Tasha's mother. "He must have fallen out of his cot again. I'll go and put him back."

Just then, a hedgehog wandered out from under a chair and stopped in the middle of the floor.

"What is that?" asked the queen. "It looks like a hedge—"

"Oh, my brush," said Tasha. "I wondered where that had got to." And she picked up the hedgehog, turned it upside down and started brushing her hair with it. "I hate to

have tangled hair, don't you, Your Majesty?"

"Indeed," said the Queen, eyeing Tasha suspiciously. "Is there any pepper?" she asked.

"Here, Your Majesty," said Tasha, placing her pet hamster in front of the queen. Hammie was wearing a little hat full of pepper with holes in the top, and he was standing as still and upright as he could, with his eyes closed.

"What a strange-looking pepper pot," said the queen, picking up Hammie and shaking him vigorously. A cloud of pepper filled the room and Hammie sneezed.

"It sneezed!" cried the queen in alarm. "I am sure the pepper pot sneezed!"

Then one of the rabbits moved. It wasn't his fault; the heavy books were leaning against him. As books tumbled off the shelf the rabbit leapt out of the way to avoid being squashed.

The queen screamed and turned to Tasha, her face red with rage.

"You know I have banned animals!" she yelled, and stamped her foot hard, right on the kangaroo's foot. That was enough for the poor kangaroo. He started bounding around the room with the queen clinging on for dear life. Squealing loudly, the pig ran off and the plates fell crashing to the floor. The cranes squawked and took off out of the window, the lampshades still on their heads. The cat cushions leapt from the chairs, the snake draught excluders slithered out of the door and the kangaroo bounded out of the house and made for the open country, with Queen Kalimena still clinging on.

"Put me down!" screamed the queen, and finally the kangaroo did – but just then, the swans decided it was time to get away. They flapped their wings and took to the air,

taking the queen with them as they flew. Higher and higher they soared.

"OHHH!" screamed the queen. Then "Oohh," in a slightly different voice. She was flying, which was something she'd always wanted to do. The swans took her high over her kingdom, beating their great white wings, and the queen laughed as she swooped low over the palace and the town.

When, finally, the swans brought the queen gently down beside the lake, she was ecstatic with joy. Her court officials ran outside.

"Shoot the swans," one of them shouted.

"No," cried the queen. "Let them live. Let all the animals live. They are wonderful."

So the swans returned to the lake, the rabbits went back to their burrows, the sheep climbed gratefully down from the trees, and they all lived properly ever after.

Princess of Hearts

Princess Ruby was given her name because she was born with ruby-red lips in the shape of a tiny heart. When she grew up she was very beautiful, with coal-black hair down to her waist, green eyes and skin as pale as milk.

She was a charming and friendly girl, but she insisted that everything she owned was heart-shaped! Her bed was heart-shaped, her table and chair were heart-shaped, her cushions were heart-shaped, even the sandwiches her maid brought her at tea time were cut into the shape of hearts!

As soon as she was old enough, the king and queen wanted Princess Ruby to find a husband.

"There is a prince in the next kingdom who is looking for a wife," they told her. "He is brave and handsome and rich. Everything a princess could wish for."

But the foolish princess declared: "I will only marry this prince if he can change the stars in the sky to hearts!"

The king and queen didn't know how to answer!

When Prince Gallant came to visit he was indeed as handsome as her parents had said. Princess Ruby liked his kindly eyes and his pleasant smile.

They spent the afternoon walking in the palace gardens, and talking about everything under the sun. But Prince Gallant could not promise Princess Ruby that he could change the shape of the stars. So the princess would not marry him!

As she watched the prince ride away, Princess Ruby suddenly wished she had not been so foolish!

Prince Gallant was unhappy, too, as he rode home through the forest.

Suddenly, he heard a screeching sound. In the clearing, a dragon was attacking a peacock.

Jumping off his horse, the prince took out his sword and chased the dragon away. The peacock was in a sorry state. All his beautiful tail feathers were scattered around him.

"Thank you for saving me," said the peacock.

The prince was astonished to hear the peacock talk.

"I have magical powers," explained the peacock. "But I am now very weak. The dragon has pulled out some of my magic feathers!"

The prince set to work gathering up all the peacock's feathers. As soon as the feathers had been returned, the peacock gave a loud cry and spread his tail wide. The peacock's tail glowed.

"Before I go, I will grant you a single wish," he told the prince. Prince Gallant wished that the stars in the sky would change into the shape of hearts!

Later that night Princess Ruby was in her bedchamber. She was beginning to regret that she had refused to marry Prince Gallant.

Feeling sad, she looked out of the window at the full moon casting its radiant light over the hills and fields beyond the palace.

Then she glanced at the stars – and she couldn't believe her eyes! Every single one was in the shape of a silver heart!

At that moment she saw Prince Gallant riding over the hill. He stopped his horse beneath Princess Ruby's window.

She was overjoyed to see him. "Will you ever forgive me," she cried, "for being so foolish as to ask you to change the shape of the stars?"

"There is nothing to forgive," said the prince, and again he asked if she would marry him. Filled with delight Princess Ruby, of course, agreed!

They were married on a lovely summer's day. And when Princess Ruby made her wedding vows, she promised never to ask for anything foolish again!

Cinderella

Once upon a time, there lived a very pretty little girl. When she was young, sadly, her mother died. Her father remarried, but the girl's stepmother was a mean woman with two ugly daughters.

These stepsisters were so jealous of the young girl's beauty that they treated her like a servant and made her

sit among the cinders in the kitchen.

They called her Cinderella, and before long everyone, even her father, had forgotten the little girl's real name.

Cinderella missed her real mother more and more each day.

One day, an invitation arrived from the royal palace. The king and queen were holding a ball for the prince's

twenty-first birthday, and all the fine ladies of the kingdom were invited.

Cinderella's stepsisters were very excited when their invitations arrived.

"I will wear my red velvet gown!" cried the first stepsister. "And the black pearl necklace that Mother gave to me."

"And I will wear my blue silk dress!" cried the other. "With a silver tiara."

"Come, Cinderella!" they called. "You must help us to get ready!"

Cinderella helped her stepsisters with their silk stockings and frilly petticoats. She brushed and curled their hair and powdered their cheeks and noses. At last, she squeezed them into their beautiful ball gowns.

But even after all this, the two ugly stepsisters weren't nearly as lovely as Cinderella was in her rags. This made them both very jealous and very angry, and they began to tease her.

"Too bad you can't come to the ball, Cinders!" sneered the first stepsister.

"Yes," laughed the other one. "They'd never let a shabby creature like you near the palace!"

Cinderella said nothing, but inside, her heart was breaking. She really wanted to go to the ball.

After her stepsisters left, she sat and wept.

"Dry your tears, my dear," said a gentle voice.

Cinderella was amazed. A kind old woman stood before her. In her hand was a sparkly wand that shone.

"I am your Fairy Godmother," she told Cinderella. "And you shall go to the ball!"

"But I have nothing to wear! And how will I get there?" cried Cinderella.

The Fairy Godmother smiled! She asked Cinders

to fetch her the biggest pumpkin in the garden. With a flick of her magic wand

she turned it into a golden carriage, and the mice in the kitchen mousetrap into fine horses. A fat rat soon became a handsome coachman.

Cinderella couldn't believe her eyes.

Smiling, the Fairy Godmother waved her wand once more and suddenly Cinders was dressed in a splendid ball gown, with sparkling glass slippers on her feet.

"My magic ends at midnight, so you must be home before then," said the Fairy Godmother.

When Cinderella arrived at the ball, everyone was dazzled by her beauty.

Whispers went round the ballroom as the other guests wondered who this enchanting stranger could be. Even Cinderella's own stepsisters did not recognise her.

As soon as the prince saw Cinderella, he fell in love with her. "Would you do me the honour of this dance?" he asked.

"Why certainly, sir," Cinderella answered. And from that moment on he only had eyes for Cinderella.

Soon the clock struck midnight. "I must go!" said Cinderella, suddenly remembering her promise to her Fairy Godmother. She fled from the ballroom and ran down the

palace steps. The prince ran after her, but when he got outside, she was gone. He didn't notice a grubby servant girl holding a pumpkin. A few mice and a rat were scurrying around her feet.

But there on the steps was one dainty glass slipper. The prince picked it up and rushed back into the palace. "Does anyone know who this slipper belongs to?" he cried.

The next day, Cinderella's stepsisters could talk of nothing but the ball, and the beautiful stranger who had danced all night with the prince. As they were talking, there was a knock at the door.

"Cinderella, quick, jump to it and see who it is." called her stepmother. Standing on the doorstep was His Highness the Prince with one of the royal footmen, who was holding the little glass slipper on a velvet cushion.

"The lady whose foot this slipper fits is my one and only true love," said the prince. "I am visiting every house in the kingdom in search of her."

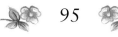

The two stepsisters began shoving each other out of the way in their rush to try on the slipper. They both squeezed and pushed as hard as they could, but their clumsy feet were far too big for the tiny glass shoe.

Then Cinderella stepped forward. "Please, Your Highness," she said shyly, "may I try?"

As her stepsisters watched in utter amazement, Cinderella slid her foot into the dainty slipper. It fitted as if it were made for her!

As the prince gazed into her eyes, he knew he had found his love – and Cinderella knew she had found hers.

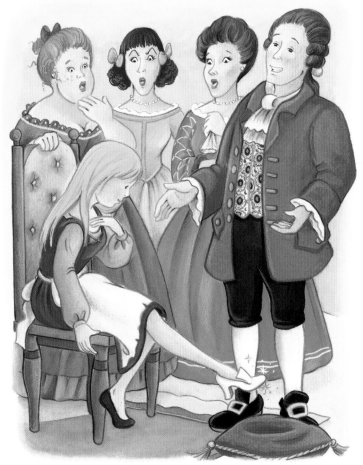

CINDERELLA

Cinderella and the prince soon set a date to be married. On the day of their wedding, the land rang with the sound of bells, and the sun shone as the people cheered. Even Cinderella's nasty stepsisters were invited. Everyone had a really wonderful day, and Cinderella and her prince lived happily ever after.

The Greek Princess and the Young Gardener

There was once an old king with one daughter. The king grew ill and it seemed as if the end of his life was coming, but he discovered that the apples from his garden made him better.

So the king became angry when a strange, brightly-coloured bird flew into his garden one evening and began to steal the apples.

The king called his gardener. "You must guard my apple tree day and night, for a bird is coming into the garden and stealing all the fruit."

"I will set my three sons to guard the tree. And if the bird comes near, they will shoot it with their bows and arrows," replied the gardener.

The gardener's eldest son stood guard by the apple tree. The night went on and soon he was asleep at the foot of the tree.

At midnight, the bird flew into the garden and removed an apple.

The king heard the bird, for he was a light sleeper, and dashed to his window. The bird was taking off with the finest apple in his beak.

"Wake up!" he shouted at the gardener's son. The lad grabbed his bow and arrow, but the bird had got away.

The next night, the gardener's second son was on guard. Again the lad was asleep when the bird came to steal an apple. Again the king roared at the gardener's boy, but the bird had flown away, and another of the king's finest, most succulent apples was gone from the tree.

The king began to despair.

On the third evening, it was the youngest son's turn. He was determined to gain credit with the king. The bird arrived as usual, and the boy let loose one arrow at the bird as it flew. The arrow didn't kill the bird, but as the arrow fell to the ground, one of the bird's feathers fell too.

The king was pleased, for the bird had not had the chance to steal an apple, and the king was fascinated by the feather. It was made of the finest beaten gold.

The king decided to catch the bird with the golden feathers. He offered half his kingdom, plus the hand of his daughter in marriage, to any man who captured the bird.

All the young men of the king's household, including the gardener's sons, wondered how they could find the bird.

The gardener's first son was out one day when he met a fox. "If you want to find the golden bird," said the fox, "go along this road and take lodging with the poor man and his wife."

So the boy went along the road, but opposite the poor man's house was a house with people drinking and dancing, and the gardener's first son went there for some fun.

The same thing happened to the gardener's second son, and he joined his brother.

When the third son met the fox, the animal gave him the same advice. Unlike his brothers, the young lad listened to what the fox had to say, and sought lodgings with the poor couple, and the next morning went on his way.

Soon he met the fox once more. "Well done for taking my advice," said the fox. "Do you know where to find the golden bird?"

"I have no idea," said the young man.

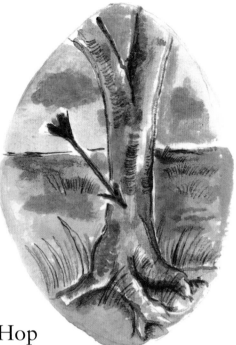

"She is in the palace of the King of Spain, some two hundred miles from here," said the fox.

The gardener's son was sad to hear that the journey was to be so long.

"Do not despair," said the fox. "Hop on my tail and, we shall soon be there."

So off they went. To the young gardener's surprise, they soon got to the King of Spain's palace. The fox turned to the lad again and told him where in the palace to find the golden bird.

"Get the bird out quickly, and do not look for other treasure," said the fox. "Then you will be safe."

The youth entered the palace and found the bird in a dull iron cage. Next to it was a fine golden cage, which the lad thought would be a better home for the marvellous bird. So he tried to tempt the creature into the golden cage. But all that happened was that the bird let out a terrible squeal, and the palace guards came running. Soon, the boy found himself in front of the King of Spain himself.

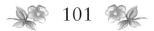

"I should hang you for a thief," said the king. "But you have a chance to win your life, and the golden bird too. Get me the bay filly belonging to the King of Morocco, a horse that runs faster than any other. Then you shall have the golden bird."

The young man found his friend the fox, and they went on their way to find the King of Morocco.

They arrived and the fox spoke sternly to the lad. "When you get into the stables, do not touch a thing. Lead out the bay filly, and all will be well."

When he entered the stable, the boy saw a fine golden saddle, much better than the leather one on the filly's back, so he decided to change it over. But palace guards appeared from every quarter, and the King of Morocco himself soon arrived.

"I should hang you for a thief," said the king. "But there is one thing that I want, and if you help me, then I will let you go, and the bay filly with you." The king explained that he wanted to marry Golden Locks, the daughter of the King of Greece, and asked the gardener's boy to go to Greece and bring back the princess.

The lad and the fox set off, and again the speed of the fox was such that by nightfall they arrived at the king's palace. "Do not let her touch anything or anyone as you come out," warned the fox.

The lad found the princess and quietly explained why he wanted to take her to Morocco. At first, she was unwilling to go with him, but as she looked at the young gardener, her heart began to melt and she agreed. "Only let me kiss my father goodbye," she said. The princess promised not to waken him, but as soon as her lips touched her father's he let out a great cry, and guards came running.

The king listened to the young gardener's story. He was sad to let his daughter go. "I will only let her go if you will clear up the great heap of clay in front of my palace," said the king. The heap had got larger every time a shovel of clay was removed.

To everyone's great astonishment, including that of the young gardener, the pile of clay was cleared. The lad knew that the fox had something to do with it. So the young gardener, the princess and the fox went on their way.

By the time they arrived at the King of Morocco's palace,

the young gardener and the princess were in love. The king brought out his bay filly in exchange for the princess, and the pair looked longingly at each other. "Please let me say farewell to the princess before I depart," said the lad.

When the king was distracted, the pair and the fox jumped up on the horse and rode off to the King of Spain's palace.

Before they entered the palace the fox said, "If you give the king the filly, I will have to carry you all home. I am not strong enough, so when you hand over the horse, go up to the creature and stroke it, as if you are saying farewell. When the king is distracted, jump on the filly's back and ride away at top speed."

The king brought out the golden bird, and gave it to the gardener's boy. Then, to his amazement, the boy rode the filly out of the palace gates where he met up with the fox and the princess again, and the three returned to the home of the young gardener.

They reached the spot where the lad and the fox first met, and the young gardener turned to the creature to thank him

for all his help.

"Now will you help me?" asked the fox. "Take your sword and chop off my head and tail."

The young man could not do this to

his friend, but his eldest brother, who knew nothing about the fox, dealt the two blows.

A young man appeared and the Greek princess recognised her brother, who had been bewitched.

The Greek princess and the young gardener were overjoyed, and they longed to share their joy with the young gardener's master, the old king. So the three of them went to see the old king and his daughter, gave the king his golden bird, and told them the whole story.

The Greek princess married the young gardener, and the Greek prince married the daughter of the old king. The king was so enchanted with his golden bird that he even shared with it some of the apples from his favourite tree.

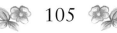

Puss in Boots

There was once a miller who had three sons. When he died, he left his mill to the eldest son, his cottage to his middle son and only his pet cat to his youngest son, William.

William went and sat under a tree, feeling very miserable and sorry for himself. "What will become of us, Puss?" he moaned.

To William's utter amazement, Puss answered him.

"Don't worry, master," said the cat. "Just do what I say and you will be far richer than either of your brothers!"

Puss told William to get him a fine suit of clothes, a pair of soft leather boots and a strong canvas sack. Then he

caught a huge rabbit, put it in the sack, and took it to the palace. No one there had ever seen a talking cat before, so he was granted an immediate audience with the king.

"Your Majesty," said Puss, "this fine rabbit is a gift from my master, the Marquis of Carabas."

The king had never heard of the Marquis of Carabas, but he was too embarrassed to admit this. "Please thank the marquis," he said to Puss, "and give him my regards."

The next day, Puss caught some plump partridges and once more he took them to the king, with the same message: "These are from my master."

For several months, Puss went on bringing the king fine gifts.

One day, he heard that the king would be riding along the river bank that afternoon with the princess.

"Master," said Puss, "you must go swimming in the river today."

"Why?" asked William.

"Just do as I say, and you will see," answered Puss.

While William was swimming, Puss hid all his clothes. Then, when he saw the king's carriage approaching, he ran up to it shouting for help.

"Help!" cried Puss. "Robbers have stolen my master's clothes!"

When the king recognised the cat, he called to his chief steward and ordered him to bring a fine new suit from the palace.

"It must be of the finest cut," said the king, "and made from the softest cloth, do you hear! Only the best

will do for the Marquis of Carabas!"

Once he was dressed in his fine new suit, William looked quite handsome. The princess invited him to join her and her father in the carriage.

As William and the princess sat side by side, they began to fall in love.

Meanwhile, Puss ran ahead until he came to a meadow where he saw some men mowing. "The king's carriage is coming," Puss told them. "When he asks whose meadow this is, say it belongs to the Marquis of Carabas – or you will have your heads cut off!"

The mowers didn't dare to disobey.

When the royal carriage came by, the king asked who the meadow belonged to. The mowers quickly replied, "The Marquis of Carabas."

"I can see that you are very well off indeed," the king said to William, who blushed modestly. That made the princess love him even more!

Down the road, Puss came to a field where men were harvesting corn.

"When the king asks whose corn this is," Puss told them, "say it belongs to the Marquis of Carabas – or you will have your heads cut off!"

The harvesters didn't dare to disobey.

Next, Puss came to an enormous castle which he knew belonged to a fierce ogre. Still he bravely knocked on the door.

When the ogre let him in, Puss bowed low and said, "I have heard that you have wondrous

powers, and can change yourself into anything – even a lion or an elephant."

"That is true," said the ogre. And to prove it, he changed himself into a snarling, growling lion.

Puss was terrified and leapt up onto a cupboard. Then the ogre changed himself back again.

"That was amazing," Puss remarked. "But surely it cannot be too difficult for someone of your size to change into a creature as big as a lion. If you were truly the magician they say you are, you could turn into something tiny – like a mouse."

"Of course I can do that!" bellowed the ogre. In an instant he became a little brown mouse scurrying across the floor.

Quick as a flash, Puss leapt off the cupboard, pounced on the mouse and ate it in one big gulp!

Soon, Puss heard the king's carriage drawing near and rushed outside. As it approached, he bowed low and said, "Welcome, Your Majesty, to the home of the Marquis of Carabas."

The king was very impressed indeed. "May we come in?" he asked William.

"Of course, Your Majesty," replied William, a little confused.

As they walked through the castle, the king was delighted to see treasures of great value everywhere he looked. He was so pleased that he said to William, "You are the perfect husband for my daughter."

William and the princess were very happy and later that day they were married. They lived in the ogre's castle happily ever after. Puss, of course, lived with them – though he never chased mice again!

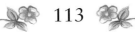

The Pig and the Jewels

aisy was as pretty as a picture. She was very kind, too. Daisy looked after all the animals on the farm where she lived. She loved them all dearly, and the animals all loved her too.

But Daisy dreamt of being more than a farmer's daughter. As she fed the hens and the ducks or counted the sheep, Daisy day-dreamed about being a princess. At night when she lay in bed she would say to herself, "Oh, how I wish I could be a princess!"

One day she found a sick pig at the edge of the forest. She carried him to the farm and nursed him until he was better. The pig became her favourite animal, and he followed her wherever she went.

She told him all her secrets, and he listened carefully, his little eyes fixed on hers. It was almost as if he understood everything she said. She even told him the most important secret of all.

"Dear little pig," she whispered in his ear, "I wish, I wish I could be a princess!"

That night the pig went away. When he returned the next morning, he had a tiara made of precious jewels on his head. The pig stood in front of Daisy, the jewels glinting in the sunshine.

"Darling pig," cried Daisy, "is that for me?" The pig grunted. Daisy took the tiara and put it on her head. It fitted her perfectly.

The next night the pig went away again. In the morning he returned as before, this time with a beautiful necklace. Daisy put it on.

"How do I look?" she asked him. But of course the pig just grunted.

After that the pig went away every night for six nights. And every morning for six mornings he returned with something different.

First he brought a dress of white silk, followed by a crimson cloak and soft leather shoes. Then bracelets set with jewels, and long lengths of satin ribbon for her hair. And, finally, a ring made of gold and rubies.

Daisy put on all the gifts the pig had brought her and stood in front of a long mirror.

"At last," she whispered to her reflection, "I look just like a real princess."

The next day the pig disappeared again. Daisy didn't worry because she knew he always returned. But days went by and then weeks, and the pig did not return. Daisy missed him more than she could say.

Summer turned to autumn, and autumn to winter. The days grew short and snow lay in deep drifts on the ground. Daisy spent the evenings sitting by the fire in her white silk dress and crimson cloak. Her heart was sad and heavy when she thought about her dear, lost pig.

"I would be happy just to remain a farmer's daughter if only he would return to me," she cried, watching the logs burn in the hearth.

Suddenly there was a noise at the door – it was the pig! With a cry of joy she bent to kiss him and, as she did, he turned into a handsome prince! Daisy gasped with amazement.

"Sweet Daisy," said the prince, taking her hand. "If it wasn't for you I would still be alone and friendless, wandering in the forest."

He explained how a wicked witch had cast a spell on him to turn him into a pig. "Your kiss broke the spell," said the prince. "Daisy, will you marry me?"

It was a dream come true. At long last, Daisy really was going to become Princess Daisy!

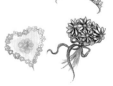

Princess Prissy and the Stinky Bog Monster

King Fusspot liked everything to be just so. Every corner of his palace was kept neat and shiny as a new pin. Each morning before breakfast he would stand at the top of the sweeping staircase that led down into the great hall, and take a royal roll-call of his entire household. If anyone was so much as one second late, they would spend the rest of the day polishing the silver.

And that was not all. The king had rules that were written in his Rule Book, a volume so heavy that three

footmen were needed to lift it. Woe betide anyone who broke his rules.

So, there was a place for everything, and everything (and everyone) was in its place.

And as long as no one stepped out of line, they all lived happily and peacefully together.

Then one morning, as King Fusspot stood at the top of the staircase as usual, taking his roll-call, something most irregular happened. He had ticked the queen and his three eldest daughters off in his register, but when he came to his youngest daughter, Princess Prissy, there was no reply!

"Princess Prissy," he called again. No answer. "Where is she?" demanded the king. "This is most unlike her."

And indeed it was, for Princess Prissy was a proper little chip off the old block. She went so far as to have her own Rule Book, covering such pressing matters as the number of brushstrokes that royal hair should receive before bed; the correct methods for tying royal ribbons; the procedure for making royal beds to ensure that no crippling lumps (in particular, peas) should endanger the royal behind, etc.

But there was nothing covering monsters, or more particularly, correct methods for monsters to carry princesses off from their beds. And even if there had been, the Stinky Bog Monster would have taken no notice. He wasn't scared of the silly old king. In fact, he wasn't scared of anyone.

So when he crashed through her window the night before, he never gave a second thought to the broken glass, crumpled covers, slimy trail, and nauseating stench he was leaving behind him, as he wrenched Princess Prissy from her bed and slung her unceremoniously over his shoulder.

He just carried her off, kicking and screaming, to his foul and stinking lair, deep in the heart of the great, dark woods, whistling merrily, with not a care in the world.

Once the Princess's absence had been noted in the king's register, the Stinky Bog Monster's trail was soon discovered.

It was obvious to all what had happened – there was no mistaking that stench!

"My poor darling daughter!" wailed the king. "Stuck in that filthy, stinking, most disorganised lair. She won't even have running water. And how can she possibly hope to survive without bath salts? Oh, it really is too terrible to contemplate!"

But fortunately for the king, help was close at hand. This was the kind of lucky break that the dashingly handsome Prince Smarmy knew was too good a chance to miss. He swiftly struck a deal with the king, ensuring the princess's hand in marriage in return for her safe rescue, and set off at once to fetch her.

Now, despite the king's thorough approval of Prince Smarmy's suave manner, pearly smile and perfectly manicured fingernails, he secretly had his doubts about the prince's ability to overcome the kind of obstacles he suspected the Stinky Bog Monster would throw in his path.

But beneath his primped and preened exterior, the prince was bold and fearless.

What is more, he was besotted with Princess Prissy, so he was not about to let anything stand in his way.

Deep in the heart of the great, dark woods, Prince Smarmy had to battle his way past demons and dragons, vampires and vipers, ogres and trolls to reach the Stinky Bog Monster's lair.

"No problem," smirked the prince smugly, brushing himself down after a rather unpleasant encounter with a three-headed beast.

And before long, he arrived at the entrance to the Stinky

Bog Monster's loathsome lair itself! Now all he had to do was retrieve the princess, whisk her back to the palace, and he'd be home, safe and up the aisle in no time.

However, Prince Smarmy, unlike the Stinky Bog Monster, was quite familiar with the princess's Rule Book (not to mention the king's) and knew all the proper procedures to follow when rescuing princesses. Most important of all, he knew he should appear on a gleaming white charger.

While he was hiding behind a tree taking the mud, gunge and bits of old troll off his horse, he caught sight of her...

She was leaning over a well, just outside the entrance to the Stinky Bog Monster's lair, pulling up a bucket of reeking, green, stagnant water. Her clothes were torn and covered in stains, her hair was a filthy, matted mess, crawling with bugs, her face was smeared with mud and grime, and her eyes gleamed and glinted wildly. But despite all this, there was no mistaking her. It really was Princess Prissy!

The prince's heart was torn with anguish. His darling princess – what had that beastly Bog Monster done to her?

Just then, as the prince prepared to leap onto his charger to rescue her, the Stinky Bog Monster himself appeared.

Princess Prissy turned and greeted him with a blackened, gappy smile.

"Hello there, Boggy darling! Come and smell how nice and stagnant the water is today! Our tea should taste really disgusting with this!"

And with that, she reached out, took his hand and planted a slobbery kiss on his cheek!

As the prince cried out in horror, the princess and her Bog Monster turned and caught sight of him.

"Oh, yuk, not you!" spat the Princess. "If you've come to rescue me, you can get lost, I'm not coming home – ever!"

"Don't be ridiculous, Prissy," cried the horrified prince. "You can't stay here. Look at yourself – you're hideous! He's got you hypnotised. But don't worry, you'll soon come to your senses—"

"Oh, but I have come to my senses,"

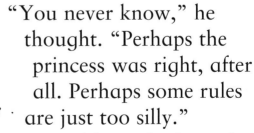

hissed Princess Prissy. "At last I've escaped all those silly rules. All that niceness, and prettiness, and good manners. I'm free! I like being rude and horrible and hideous, it's really rather fun. I've got my darling Stinky Bog Monster to thank for it, and you're too late – we got married last night!" Then Princess Prissy and the Bog Monster let out cackling laughs and staggered back inside.

There was nothing else for it. Prince Smarmy had to admit defeat, turn on his heels, and head home. He wondered what the king would say. It would certainly mess up his neat register.

Then he noticed a deep, muddy puddle in front of him.

"Why not?" he thought, and rode his clean, white horse straight through it, splattering both of them with black, sticky mud.

Then he saw another one. This time he made his horse jump into it. He laughed out loud.

"You never know," he thought. "Perhaps the princess was right, after all. Perhaps some rules are just too silly."

And he rode through every single puddle until he got back to the castle.

Princess Rosebud

In a beautiful palace in a land far away, lived a little princess. The king and queen called her Princess Rosebud, because on her left ankle was a small pink mark in the shape of a rose.

On her third birthday, Princess Rosebud was given a pretty white pony. The princess rode her pony with her nanny and her groom at her side. They went to the edge of the forest, then stopped for a rest. The pretty white pony was tied to a tree branch. The nanny and the groom talked together, while the little princess wandered along a forest path collecting flowers and leaves. They didn't notice how far the little princess had wandered.

Soon Princess Rosebud couldn't see her nanny or her groom or her beautiful white pony. She called and called for her nanny.

But no one came. It began to get dark. Princess Rosebud was scared and began to cry; she walked on until she saw a light through the trees. There was a little house with a straw roof and tiny little windows and a small wooden door.

Suddenly, the door opened, and there stood a little old woman!

Now, the old woman was blind and couldn't see the little princess, but she could hear a small child crying. The old woman was kind. She took the little princess inside and sat her by a warm fire. Then she gave her thin slices of bread and honey, and a glass of milk.

"What is your name, child?" she asked.

"Rosebud," answered the princess.

"Where do you live, child?" she asked.

"I don't know," answered the princess. "I got lost in the forest when I was walking."

"Well, you can stay with me until someone comes to find you, my dear," said the kind old woman.

Back at the palace, the king and queen were very upset that their only daughter was lost. They offered a reward of a hundred gold coins to anyone who could find her. But many years went by and no one found the little princess. The king and queen thought they would never see the princess again.

Meanwhile Rosebud was very happy living in the forest. She forgot that she had ever been a princess. She forgot she had lived in a palace. She forgot her fine clothes and jewels. She even forgot her white pony.

One day, when she was walking in the garden, a pony galloped into view. He was as white as milk, and had a jewelled saddle and bridle.

Rosebud loved the pony straight away. She climbed into the saddle, and the pony turned swiftly, and galloped off. He took her to the palace gate. Rosebud felt she had seen the palace before, but could not remember when.

Before dark, the pony returned her to the cottage in the forest.

The next day he came again, and again they visited the palace before returning to the cottage.

Then the next day, the palace gate was open. The pony trotted through the gate just as the king and queen were walking in the gardens. They saw the little girl and the pony and thought she was the prettiest girl they had ever seen.

"What is your name, child?" the queen asked her.

"Rosebud, Your Majesty," Rosebud replied.

"Ah," sighed the queen sadly, "that is the name of my long-lost daughter."

Then, just as Rosebud was mounting the pony to ride home, the queen noticed the pink rose on her left ankle! She stared at it in disbelief!

"Sire!" she cried to the king. "It is our daughter, Princess Rosebud."

The whole kingdom rejoiced to hear that the princess had returned. The king offered the old woman a reward for caring for the princess, but she shook her head.

"I only want to be near Rosebud for the rest of my days," she said.

And so the old woman came to live in the palace with Princess Rosebud.

A Knight to Remember

ong, long ago, when kings ruled over kingdoms, fearsome dragons terrorised the lands and beautiful princesses swooned over dashing knights in shining armour, there lived a very worried man called Alfred Ramsbottom. Alfred was a great big bear of a man, with an important job working as chief blacksmith to the king. He shod the king's horses, and equipped his knights with swords, shields and suits of armour.

Business had been very good recently because the kingdom where Alfred lived was being menaced by a large and loathsome dragon, who had seen off every valiant knight that had set out to slay him. Alfred could barely keep up with the workload, as knight after knight prepared to be sent into battle. Things were so bad that the king had to put up a banner on the castle walls, which read:

Knights wanted. Must be brave, dashing and fearless. Experience in dragon-slaying an advantage. Competitive salary, plus the hand of the princess upon defeat of the dragon. All eligible young men should apply to the castle at the earliest opportunity.

But there had only been three applicants. They had all made very tasty breakfasts for the dragon, who was looking forward to more.

So, you are probably wondering, just what was worrying Alfred? Was it the heavy workload? Was it the dragon? Was he worried that the king would send him out to slay the dragon? Well, you won't be able to guess, so I'll tell you… it was his son, Nigel.

Now, Nigel was as different from his dad as it was possible to be. He was small, he was weedy, he had soft, smooth hands. Worse still, he liked music, and poetry and… knitting! He'd happily sit by the fire with his mother for hours on end, needles clicking away as he knitted himself a nice new tunic.

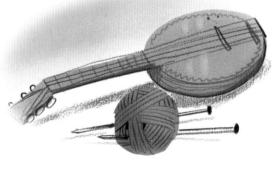

There was no chance of him joining the family business – he couldn't even lift his father's hammers!

Just the night before, Nigel had overheard his parents talking:

"What will become of the boy?" groaned Alfred. "All he does is sit around the house all day singing and playing his lute. And as for the knitting – what good is that going to do him? How will he ever be able to make his way in the world?"

"Now, now, dear," soothed his wife. "Don't worry. We mustn't lose hope. He may surprise us yet!"

Poor Nigel, being the sensitive chap that he was, was mortified to discover that he was a disappointment to his parents, and he decided to give them the surprise of their lives!

Nigel had seen the king's advertisement, and while he'd been knitting, he'd been thinking. He wasn't big and butch, but he was quick and clever. He'd come up with a plan to outsmart that mean old dragon, and now was the time to put it into action…

The king could hardly keep a straight face when Nigel presented himself at court, bowed low before the throne and declared himself at the king's service.

What hope did a measly little shrimp like this have of defeating the dragon? Still, beggars can't be choosers, thought the king, and in the absence of other offers, he took up his sword and knighted Nigel without delay.

"Good luck," smiled the princess, peeping out shyly from behind her father's throne. She rather liked the look of this one. He was a change from the great hairy brutes she'd seen so far.

Alfred was shocked when Nigel presented himself and his horse to be kitted out for battle. He really had something to worry about now! But for all his worries about his son, he loved him dearly, and begged him to reconsider.

"How can you hope to win?" Alfred pleaded. "You'll be a bite-sized snack for this dragon!"

"Don't worry, Dad," soothed Nigel. "You want me to make my way in the world – and that's just what I intend to do! Besides, I have a cunning plan!"

With a mysterious smile, he opened his knapsack to reveal his lute, two large knitting needles and a huge ball of wool! Poor Alfred looked at his son in puzzlement and dismay, but before he had time to ask questions, Nigel leapt onto his horse and rode away into the forest.

For four long days and nights nothing more was heard of him.

While his parents sat anxiously at home, Nigel was very busy indeed. When he arrived at the dragon's lair, he hid himself in a small crack in the rock at the mouth of the dragon's cave. He waited till he heard the dragon snoring away deep in the depths, then took out his knitting needles and the huge ball of wool. His needles flashed as he worked furiously, and in no time at all he had knitted a huge net that stretched across the entire mouth of the cave.

Then he took out his lute and, perching high on a rock above the cave, he began to play the sweetest song he knew.

Now, not many people know this, but dragons can't stand music or poetry. It jangles their nerves, and their skin crawls and their teeth grind.

But Nigel knew, so it was no surprise to him that his plan worked like a dream.

On hearing the gentle melody, the dragon came roaring towards the mouth of the cave, nostrils flaring and flames shooting, which is just what Nigel had hoped he'd do.

The flames singed a hole in the middle of the net, which was just big enough for the dragon's head to slip through as he charged towards it. Before he knew where he was, the net had slipped over him like a jumper, and he was well and truly tangled up and held fast.

He writhed and struggled, but Nigel's knitting held firm! Then came the next part of the plan.

With the dragon held captive, Nigel took up his lute once more, and serenaded him with the soppiest, silliest love songs he knew. And when he got bored, he recited poetry –

long odes to lost loves that drove the dragon to distraction.

For four days and nights Nigel kept up his performance, until the demented dragon could stand it no more, and begged Nigel to let him flee the kingdom to escape. Nigel kept on singing while he cut through the net, and the last time he saw the dragon, he was tearing across the distant hills, howling and holding his ears.

Nigel rode home triumphantly, and as you can imagine, the king was delighted. So was the princess, who whisked him up the aisle as fast as you can say knit one, purl one.

As for Alfred, well, his worries were over at last. Nigel had made his mark as a knight to remember, and in the process had landed himself the perfect position in life, as a prince with nothing better to do than to spend his days singing, playing his lute and knitting. And he kept the princess in lovely jumpers. Perfect!

The Enchanted Garden

Princess Sylvie grew up in a beautiful castle, but it had no garden. So she loved to walk through the meadows just to look at the flowers. Princess Sylvie loved flowers!

One day Princess Sylvie found an overgrown path. She asked a woman where the path led.

"That path leads to the garden of the enchantress!" said the woman.

"What is an enchantress?" Princess Sylvie asked.

"Someone who uses magic! So be warned… don't pick the flowers or who knows what terrible things might happen!"

Princess Sylvie followed the path until she came to a small cottage with the prettiest garden she had ever seen. It was filled with flowers of every colour and perfume!

After that, Princess Sylvie went every day. Winter came and snow lay thick, yet the garden stayed the same.

Princess Sylvie forgot all about the enchantress. One wintry day, she picked a rose from the garden and took it back to the castle. As she put it in water, Princess Sylvie suddenly remembered the warning. She'd picked a flower from the enchanted garden and who knew what terrible things might happen?

But days passed and nothing happened. The rose stayed as fresh as the day it was picked.

Then months passed and still nothing happened. Forgetting her fears, Princess Sylvie decided to go back to the enchanted garden.

When she saw the garden, Princess Sylvie wanted to cry. The grass was brown. The flowers had withered and died. Then she heard someone weeping.

Inside the cottage the enchantress was sitting by the fire, crying. She was old and bent. Although Princess Sylvie was afraid, she felt sorry for her.

"What happened to your garden?" Princess Sylvie asked.

"Someone picked a rose from my magic garden!" said the enchantress. "The rose will live for ever, but the rest must die!"

"Can't your magic bring the garden back to life?" Princess Sylvie asked.

"Alas, when the rose was picked, my magic was lost. And now, I too will wither and die."

"What can I do?" asked Princess Sylvie, heartbroken.

"Only a princess can bring my magic back," she replied.

"How?" asked Princess Sylvie.

"She must bring me six sacks full of stinging nettles. No princess would do such a thing."

Princess Sylvie didn't say anything. She turned and ran to the meadow. She gathered up armful after armful of nettles, not caring that they stung her. She filled six sacks and took them back to the enchantress.

"You are kind," she said. "But the nettles must be picked by a princess."

"But I am a princess," said Princess Sylvie.

Without delay, the enchantress made a magic potion with the nettles and drank it. Instantly, the garden became enchanted again! Princess Sylvie gasped. Gone was the bent old lady and in her place was a young woman.

"My beautiful garden is restored," smiled the enchantress, "and so am I!"

And so the enchantress and the princess became great friends and shared the enchanted garden.

Rapunzel

Once upon a time there lived a couple who after many years, found they were expecting a baby.

Their tiny cottage stood next to a river. Across the river was a beautiful garden full of glorious flowers and tasty-looking vegetables.

One day, the woman looked across the river and saw a vegetable called rampion growing in the garden. It looked delicious, and she longed to taste it. She begged her husband to get some for her.

The garden belonged to an evil witch, and the husband refused. But his wife would eat nothing else,

and grew thin and pale. At last he agreed, so that night, the man crossed the river, and picked handfuls of rampion from the witch's garden.

Suddenly the evil witch appeared. "How dare you steal from me!" she roared.

"F-Forgive me," the man stammered. "My wife is expecting a baby and longed for some of this vegetable. If she doesn't have it, I'm afraid that she will die."

"Very well," said the witch, "take all you want. But you must give me something in return. When your baby is born, I must have it."

Terrified, the man agreed and fled.

The wife was overjoyed and made a salad with the rampion. She ate it hungrily.

After that, the man went to the witch's garden every day. He brought home baskets of rampion, and his wife grew strong and healthy.

A few months later she gave birth to a beautiful baby girl.

The man had forgotten all about his promise to the witch, but when the baby was just a day old, the witch burst in and took her away. The baby's parents were heartbroken and never saw her or the witch again.

The witch called the baby Rapunzel. She took her to a cottage deep in a forest, and took good care of her.

On Rapunzel's twelfth birthday, the cruel witch imprisoned her in a forbidding high tower, with no doors and just one small window at the very top.

Every day the witch came and stood at the bottom of the tower, and called,

"Rapunzel, Rapunzel!
Let down your long hair!"

RAPUNZEL

Rapunzel would let down her long, golden hair, and the witch would begin to climb up.

Rapunzel spent many lonely years in her tower. To pass the time, she often sat by the window and sang.

One day, a prince rode through the forest. Enchanted by

the sound of Rapunzel's sweet voice, the young prince followed it until he came to the doorless tower.

Just then the witch arrived. The prince quickly hid as she called: "*Rapunzel, Rapunzel! Let down your long hair!*"

The witch climbed up the hair, and the prince knew that this was the way he would be able to meet the owner of the beautiful voice.

After the witch had gone, the prince stood beneath the tower and called out in a voice like the witch's:

"Rapunzel, Rapunzel!
Let down your long hair!"

When Rapunzel's golden hair came tumbling down, he climbed up to the window.

Rapunzel was frightened when she saw the prince. But he was gentle and kind, and she quickly lost her fear.

The prince came to see Rapunzel often, and they soon fell in love. He asked her to marry him – but how would Rapunzel leave the tower?

Rapunzel had an idea. "Each time you visit," she told the prince, "bring me a ball of strong silk. I will plait it into a long, long ladder. When it is finished I will climb down and run away to marry you."

The prince did as Rapunzel asked, and soon the ladder was ready.

But on the very day she was to run away, something terrible happened. When the witch climbed through the window, Rapunzel absent-mindedly said, "Why do you pull so hard at my hair? The prince is not so rough." Suddenly, Rapunzel realised what she had said.

The witch flew into a raging fury. "You ungrateful little wretch!" she screamed. "I have protected you from the world, and you have betrayed me. Now you must be punished!"

"I'm sorry," Rapunzel sobbed, as she fell to her knees. "I didn't mean to make you cross."

The witch grabbed a pair of scissors and – snip-snap-snip-snap – cut off Rapunzel's long golden hair. Then, using the ladder to climb down, the witch carried Rapunzel off to a faraway land, where she left her to wander all alone without any food, water or anything to keep her warm.

That evening, when the prince called, the witch let down Rapunzel's hair. The prince climbed quickly up, and couldn't believe his eyes!

"The bird has flown, my pretty!" the witch cackled evilly. "You will never see Rapunzel again!"

Overcome with grief, the sad prince threw himself from the tower. His fall was broken by some brambles, but they also scratched and blinded him.

The prince stumbled away and wandered the land for a year, living on berries and rainwater.

Then one day the prince heard a beautiful sound – the sweet voice of Rapunzel! He called her name and she ran

into his arms, weeping tears of joy. The tears fell onto the prince's wounded eyes and suddenly he could see again.

The prince took Rapunzel home to his castle, where they were married and lived happily ever after.

The Dog with No Voice

There once lived a prince whose words were pure poetry. He amused the court with his witty, rhyming verse, yet his kind and thoughtful words made him popular with all. It was said he could even charm the birds from the trees.

One day, he was walking in the forest when he came upon an old lady with a huge bundle on her back. "Let me help," said the prince. He took the load and walked along beside the woman. They chatted away and before long they had reached the old lady's door.

Now the old lady – who was really a witch – had been listening intently to the prince's words. "What a fine voice he has!" she thought to herself. "I would like my own son to speak like that. Then maybe he could find himself

a wealthy wife and we'd be rich for evermore!"

"You must be thirsty," she said to the prince. "Let me give you something to quench your

thirst, to repay you for your kindness." The prince gratefully accepted, and was given a delicious drink which he drained to the last drop. He was about to thank the witch when he began to feel very peculiar. He found he was getting smaller and smaller. He looked down at his feet and saw two hairy paws. Then he turned round and saw to his horror that he had grown a shaggy tail! He tried to shout at the witch but all that came out of his mouth was a loud bark!

The witch hugged herself for joy. "My spell worked!" she cackled. "Come here, my son!" she called.

There appeared at the door a rough-looking young man. "What's going on, my dearest mother?" he said, in a voice that sounded familiar to the prince. Then he looked down and exclaimed, "Where did you find this poor little dog?"

Now the prince understood what had happened. "The old lady has turned me into a humble hound and given my voice to her son. Whatever am I to do?" he thought miserably.

"I can't return to the palace. They'll never let a stray dog in." He turned with his tail between his legs and trotted off forlornly into the forest.

The witch and her son were delighted with his new voice. She made him scrub himself clean from top to toe and dressed him in the prince's clothes. "Now go," she said, "and don't return until you've found a rich girl to marry!"

The young man set off, eager to try out his new voice. Soon he was feeling very pleased with himself as he talked to passers-by. "What a very polite young man!" and "What a wonderful way with words," folk cried. "He could charm the birds out of the trees," other people said.

The witch's son travelled far and wide until at last he came to a castle where he spied a fair princess sitting on her balcony. He called to her and straight away she arose and looked down into the garden, enraptured by the sound of his beautiful voice. She was enchanted by his fine words and guessed they must belong to a prince.

Soon the princess and the witch's son were chatting away merrily, and to his delight, when he asked her to marry him she readily agreed. "For one with so beautiful a voice," she thought to herself, "must indeed be a fine young man."

Meanwhile, the poor dog-prince wandered in the forest, surviving as best he could by foraging for roots and fruits in the undergrowth. Feeling truly miserable, he stopped to drink from a stream. As he dipped his long dog's tongue in the cool water, he caught sight of someone sitting on a bridge. It was a pixie, fishing with a tiny net.

"Cheer up!" said the little fellow, "I saw everything that happened and I think I know how we can get your voice back. Follow me!" And with that he was off, dancing away through the forest with the dog-prince trotting along behind.

They seemed to go on forever, and the dog-prince was feeling very hot. The pads of his paws were quite sore by the time they reached the castle.
He could see the witch's son in the garden calling to the princess on the balcony. The dog-prince's eyes suddenly filled with tears.

She was quite the loveliest girl he had ever seen and he wished he could marry her himself.

"We will be married today," the witch's son was saying in the prince's voice, "I will await you by the church, my fairest one." Seizing his fishing net, the pixie leapt high in the air. As the words "my fairest one" floated up to the balcony, he caught them in the net and gave them back to the dog-prince.

As soon as he had swallowed the words, the dog-prince could speak again. "Thank you, little pixie," he cried, "but what can I do? Now I am a dog with a prince's voice. The princess will never marry me."

"If you want to break the witch's spell, you must go to the church – fast!" said the pixie. And with those words he disappeared.

Straight away, the dog-prince ran to the church door. There was the princess looking most perplexed, for standing beside her was the witch's son – with not a word in his head.

"I don't understand," she cried,

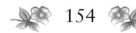

"I thought I was to marry a silver–tongued young man, but now I find he is a dumb ragamuffin!"

"I can explain," exclaimed the dog-prince.

The princess spun around. "Who can explain?" she asked, for all she could see was a dog in front of her. "What a handsome dog!" she cried, bending down and kissing him on the nose. To her astonishment, the dog's hairy paws and shaggy tail immediately disappeared and there stood the prince. "But you're... but he..." she stammered, looking from the prince to the witch's son.

Well, the prince explained everything that had happened, and after that he and the princess were married with great rejoicing. And as for the witch's son? He wasn't a bad young man, really, so the prince taught him to speak again – with a beautiful voice – and he married the princess's younger sister.

I Don't Know

Once, a duke who lived in Brittany was riding home with his manservant when they saw a young child lying asleep, alone by the side of the road. The duke was sad to see a boy, about five years old, by the roadside, so he got down from his horse, and woke him up.

"Who left you here, my boy?" asked the duke.

"I don't know."

"Who are your parents?"

"I don't know."

"Which town do you come from?"

"I don't know."

"What are you called?"

"I don't know."

"No one seems to be taking care of you. We will take you home and keep you safe." So the duke took the child to his castle, and called him N'oun-Doaré, which is the Breton for "I don't know."

N'oun-Doaré grew up with the family and was a healthy, intelligent child. He was sent away to school and became a handsome young man.

I Don't Know

When N'oun-Doaré was eighteen, the duke brought him back to live at the castle, and, to show N'oun-Doaré how pleased he was with his progress, took him to the local fair to buy him his own sword and his own horse.

First they went to look for a horse. There were many horse-dealers at the fair, but N'oun-Doaré could find no steed that suited him. Then they met a man leading an old mare and N'oun-Doaré shouted, "Yes! That is the horse I want!"

The duke was surprised. "That old nag?" he said. But the boy insisted.

The horse's owner spoke quietly to N'oun-Doaré. "Your choice is good. See the knots in the mare's mane? Undo one of them, and she will fly fifteen hundred leagues through the air."

Then the duke and N'oun-Doaré visited the armourer. But again, no sword was right – then N'oun-Doaré saw an old, rusty sword. "That is the sword I would like."

"But you deserve much better than that," said the duke. "It is old and rusty."

"Please buy it for me; I will put it to good use."

So they bought the old sword. When the lad looked closely at the sword he saw an inscription, almost covered by rust, which said, "I am invincible."

N'oun-Doaré could not wait to try a magical flight with his mare, and soon he undid one of the knots in her mane.

They flew to Paris, where N'oun-Doaré marvelled at the city's sights.

By chance the duke was also there – he had been called to attend the king. When he met the boy, they went to the royal palace together.

The duke introduced N'oun-Doaré to the king, and the lad was given a job looking after some of the royal stables.

One night, N'oun-Doaré was passing a crossroads when he saw something glint in the moonlight. It was a crown encrusted with diamonds that shone in the dark. A voice suddenly said, "Be on your guard if you take that." N'oun-Doaré did not realise, but it was actually the voice of his old mare. N'oun-Doaré paused, then took it with him.

He told no one about the crown and hid it in the stables, but two of the other servants saw it shining through the keyhole and went to tell the king.

The king took the crown and called all his wise men about him. But none of them knew where it had come from. There was an inscription on the crown in a strange language which no one could read.

Then a child spoke up, saying that the crown belonged to the Princess of the Golden Fleece. The king turned to N'oun-Doaré: "Bring me the Princess of the Golden Fleece to be my wife, otherwise you will meet your death."

The lad got on his mare and began to search for the princess, although he had little idea about where to look. He came to a beach, and saw a fish, stuck on the sand, which seemed to be dying. "Put it in the sea," said the mare, and N'oun-Doaré did so.

"Great thanks to you," said the fish. "You have saved the life of the king of the fish."

Later they came to a bird which was trapped in a snare. "Let it go," said the mare, and N'oun-Doaré did so.

"Great thanks to you," said the bird. "You have saved the life of the king of the birds."

Later on their journey they came to a great castle, and nearby a man was chained to a tree. "Set him free," said the mare, and N'oun-Doaré did so.

"Great thanks to you. You have saved the life of the Demon King."

"Whose castle is this?" asked N'oun-Doaré.

"It belongs to the Princess of the Golden Fleece," replied the Demon King.

They went into the castle and N'oun-Doaré explained why he had come. The princess was reluctant to go, but N'oun-Doaré tricked her onto his horse, and they flew to Paris. The king wanted to marry without delay.

"Before I marry, I must have my own ring," said the princess.

N'oun-Doaré was asked to bring the ring to the king, but N'oun-Doaré had no idea where to look. Then the mare whispered, "Ask the king of the birds, who you saved. He will help you."

The king of the birds chose the wren, and told her to bring the ring to the princess. "The wren is the best bird for this task," he explained. "She can fly through the keyhole of the princess's chamber."

The wren returned with the ring, and the king wanted to marry straight away. But the princess had another demand.

"I need to have my own castle brought to me," she said.

Again, N'oun-Doaré was in despair.

Again, the mare whispered to him, "Ask the Demon King, who you saved. He will help you."

The Demon King set a whole army of demons to work, moving the castle to Paris. Then the princess had one final demand. "I do not have a key to my castle, it was dropped into the sea when we flew to Paris on N'oun-Doaré's mare."

N'oun-Doaré saw that this was a task for the king of the fish. And with that, a fish arrived with the diamond-studded key in its mouth.

At last the Princess agreed to marry the king. The guests were amazed to see N'oun-Doaré take his mare into the church. When the king and princess were married, the mare vanished, and there stood a beautiful young woman. "Please marry me, N'oun-Doaré," she said. "I am the daughter of the King of Tartary."

N'oun-Doaré and the princess set off to Tartary. People say they lived happily ever after there, but they were never seen in Brittany again.

King Pong

There once lived a king who was very fond of gardening. The royal garden was the talk of the kingdom, and the king spent most of his time tending the royal blooms. They were the most magnificent flowers you could ever imagine. There were vibrant violets, delicate delphiniums, marvellous marigolds and even lovely ruby red roses. The king could grow just about anything, and everyone said that he had green fingers, but this was largely due to the fact that he never washed his hands.

The king never had a bath either – the royal tub was full of plant pots and manure, but as the king lived all by himself this did not really matter.

The king was a handsome king. A charming king. A wise and talented king. A king with his own castle, his own teeth and his own hair. In fact he had everything a king could wish for – well almost. He did not have a queen: a royal companion who could help him rule the kingdom and spend the royal fortune. His courtiers said he was just unlucky and hadn't met Princess Right yet, but no one dared to tell him the truth – the truth being that he smelt absolutely terrible!

One day the king was in his garden tending his beloved blooms when he was suddenly overwhelmed by a feeling of loneliness and despair. His garden was far too big and far too beautiful to be enjoyed alone. So at that very moment, well, just after he'd watered his sweet peas, he decided that he would find himself a queen.

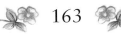

That very afternoon the king took the royal rose pruners and snipped and snipped until he had a basket filled to the brim with glorious ruby red roses. He then ordered a single red rose to be sent to every eligible princess in the kingdom. Each magnificent rose was to be accompanied by a gold-edged invitation requesting the pleasure of the company of the princess in question. The roses and the invitations were duly despatched and the king retired to his potting shed to wait.

But alas, although the rich velvety petals and sweet scent of the roses enticed each princess to make the journey to the king's castle, none were able to travel further than the front gate, so appalling was the smell that wafted towards their delicate regal nostrils.

The king was about to give up hope of ever finding a queen when, one day, a small neatly wrapped parcel arrived with the royal breakfast tray.

Inside was a tiny bottle of vibrant orange liquid and a short, handwritten note, which read:

Her Royal Highness regrets that she is unable to accept your invitation, but thanks you for the delightful rose, which did, incidentally, have a touch of greenfly.

Her Royal Highness has therefore taken the liberty of enclosing an excellent preparation which should combat this.

The king was intrigued. The very next day he ordered that one dozen royal red roses, minus greenfly, of course, be despatched directly to the princess with another invitation, asking if she would join him for afternoon tea on Tuesday at four o'clock prompt.

The next morning the king received a neatly wrapped parcel containing a splendid Savoy cabbage and a short, handwritten note which read:

Her Royal Highness thanks you most sincerely for the generous bouquet and trusts that you will accept this cabbage as a token of her appreciation. Sadly she is unable to accept your offer of tea.

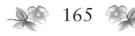

Well, by now the king was in a right royal state. He ordered one hundred ruby red roses to be sent along with a telegram demanding that the elusive princess join him for dinner that very evening – and he would not take no for an answer. Later that day a short, handwritten note arrived explaining that the princess was a little busy right now but hoped that the king would enjoy the enclosed courgettes with his dinner.

By this time however, the king was distraught, so he ordered a carriage to take him immediately – well, after his dinner, as it was a pity to waste the courgettes – to the princess's castle where he might meet her in person.

The journey was a long and tiring one and the king was relieved when, early the following morning, the horses

pulled up outside the gates of the princess's castle.

The king clambered out and gazed at the crumbling towers that held the crumbling walls of the castle together. It was very, very run down. The gates were rusty and one was hanging off its hinges.

Unperturbed, the king walked up the uneven muddy driveway and knocked at the rotten front door of the castle. There was no reply, so he knocked again and he would have knocked a third time but the knocker came off in his hand, so he decided to try round the back instead.

He passed through a rickety wooden door set in an ancient moss-covered wall and found himself in the most fantastic vegetable garden he had ever seen.

There were marrows bigger than carriages, great fat pea pods, ready to burst, cabbages, cauliflowers and lettuces, all growing in perfectly straight lines and in such abundance it took your breath away.

At the far end of the garden he saw a figure effortlessly pulling up bunches of enormous juicy carrots and throwing them into the basket by her side. She was tall and very strong. Her hair was the colour of the carrots and hung in unruly curls about her grubby face. Her patched trousers were held up with string. She paused to wipe her nose on her sleeve and it was love at first sight.

The king gave a little cough to attract her attention. The vision of loveliness looked up and the king walked steadily over to her, not noticing that she didn't smell particularly nice. He bowed politely and kissed her grimy hand. The princess blushed the colour

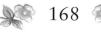

of the wonderful beetroots that were sitting in her basket.

"I'm so glad you came," she said, offering him a radish. "It's been lonely since the staff left."

"You're very beautiful," the king told her, and he meant it. The princess smiled a shy smile. "Oh you're just being nice," she said. "I'm afraid I've been so wrapped up in the garden I've rather neglected myself."

"Nonsense," said the king. "You are by far the prettiest flower in your garden."

"You are very kind," said the princess – who was far too polite to point out that she only grew vegetables.

The king then knelt in the slimy green mud to propose. Princess Composta, for that was her name, accepted without hesitation.

"We must be married at once," announced the king, and so they were – well, after he'd helped her dig up the spuds.

And they both lived smellily ever after.

Princess Petal

Princess Petal lives in a shiny white castle, surrounded by beautiful gardens, filled with pretty flowers and colourful butterflies. The princess's best friend is Sparkle, a sweet little puppy. Every morning, he helps the princess to choose her dress.

"Which one today?" she asks.

Sparkle stands next to a pretty yellow one, wags his tail and barks.

"Perfect," says the princess.

Then they play games in the garden. They love to run and jump and play Catch the Ball.

Today, Princess Petal is very excited. She has just received an invitation to a special party – a ball at the palace.

"The prince is very handsome," Petal says to her puppy. "I must look my best."

She slips on a beautiful pink dress, trimmed with jewels and satin ribbons. On her feet are dainty gold slippers. Then Petal opens her jewellery box and takes out a pair of crystal earrings and a diamond tiara.

She places the tiara carefully on her head – now she can go to the ball in her beautiful horse-drawn carriage.

As the Princess and Sparkle enter the crowded ballroom, everyone gasps in delight. The handsome prince takes the princess's hand.

"You are the loveliest lady here," he says. "May I have this dance?"

"Of course, Your Majesty!" says the princess.

Princess Petal is the happiest girl in the whole kingdom.

Now, in the crowd of people gathered at the edge of the field was a little girl. People were pushing and shoving and she couldn't see anything at all. At last, her father lifted her high up on his shoulders so that she could see into the field.

"Oh!" exclaimed the little girl in a very big voice. "So that's the red daffodil. I think it's really beautiful. What a lucky daffodil to be so different."

She slips on a beautiful pink dress, trimmed with jewels and satin ribbons. On her feet are dainty gold slippers. Then Petal opens her jewellery box and takes out a pair of crystal earrings and a diamond tiara.

She places the tiara carefully on her head – now she can go to the ball in her beautiful horse-drawn carriage.

As the Princess and Sparkle enter the crowded ballroom, everyone gasps in delight. The handsome prince takes the princess's hand.

"You are the loveliest lady here," he says. "May I have this dance?"

"Of course, Your Majesty!" says the princess.

Princess Petal is the happiest girl in the whole kingdom.

The Red Daffodil

It was spring time and all the daffodils were pushing their heads up towards the warmth of the sun. Slowly, their golden petals unfolded to let their yellow trumpets dance in the breeze. One particular field of daffodils was a blaze of gold like all the others – but right in the middle was a single splash of red, for there in the middle was a red daffodil.

From the moment she opened her petals, the red daffodil knew she was different from the other flowers. They sneered at her and whispered to each other. "What a strange, poor creature!" said one.

"She must envy our beautiful golden colour," said another.

And indeed it was true. The red daffodil wished very much that she was like the others. Instead of being proud of her red petals, she was ashamed and hung her head low.

"What's wrong with me?" she thought. "Why aren't there any other red daffodils in the field?"

Passers-by stopped to admire the field of beautiful daffodils. "What a wonderful sight!" they exclaimed. And the daffodils' heads swelled with pride and danced in the breeze all the more merrily.

Then someone spotted the red daffodil right in the middle of the field. "Look at that extraordinary flower!" the man shouted. Everyone peered into the centre of the field.

"You're right," said someone else, "there's a red daffodil in the middle." Soon a large crowd had gathered, all pointing and laughing at the red daffodil.

She could feel herself blushing even redder at the attention. "How I wish my petals would close up again," she said to herself in anguish. But try as she might, her fine red trumpet stood out for all to see.

Now, in the crowd of people gathered at the edge of the field was a little girl. People were pushing and shoving and she couldn't see anything at all. At last, her father lifted her high up on his shoulders so that she could see into the field.

"Oh!" exclaimed the little girl in a very big voice. "So that's the red daffodil. I think it's really beautiful. What a lucky daffodil to be so different."

And do you know, other people heard what the little girl said and they began to whisper to each other, "Well, I must say, I actually thought myself it was rather pretty, you know." Before long, people were praising the daffodil's beauty and saying it must be a very special flower. The red daffodil heard what the crowd was saying. Now she was blushing with pride and held her head as high as all the other daffodils in the field.

The other daffodils were furious. "What a foolish crowd," said one indignantly. "We are the beautiful ones!" They turned their heads away from the red daffodil and ignored her. She began to feel unhappy again.

By now word had spread far and wide about the amazing red daffodil and people came from all over the land to see her. Soon, the king's daughter got to hear about the red daffodil. "I must see this for myself," said the princess. She set off with her servant and eventually they came to the field where the red daffodil grew.

When the princess saw her, she clapped her hands with glee.

"The red daffodil is more beautiful than I ever imagined," she cried. Then she had an idea. "Please bring my pet dove," she said to her servant. The man looked rather puzzled, but soon he returned with the bird. "As you know," said the princess to the servant, "I am to be married tomorrow and I would dearly love to have that red daffodil in my wedding bouquet."

The princess sent the dove into the middle of the field and it gently picked up the daffodil in its beak and brought her back to where the princess stood. The princess carried the daffodil back to the palace. She put the daffodil in a vase of water and there she stayed until the next day.

In the morning, the princess's servant took the red daffodil to the church. She could hear the bells and see all the guests assembling for the wedding ceremony. Then she saw the princess arrive in a coach driven by four white horses. How lovely the princess looked in her white gown, her head crowned with deep red roses.

As the servant reached the church door, the princess's lady-in-waiting stepped forward holding a huge bouquet of flowers into which she placed the red daffodil, just as the flowers were handed to the princess.

For a while, the red daffodil was overcome by the powerful scents of the other flowers in the bouquet, but when at last she looked around her she realised, with astonishment, that all of them were red. There were red daisies, red lilies, red carnations and red foxgloves. "Welcome," said one of the daisies, "you're one of us." And for the first time in her life, the red daffodil felt really at home.

After the wedding, the princess scattered the flowers from her bouquet among the flowers in her garden. Every spring, when she opened her petals, the red daffodil found she was surrounded by lots of other red flowers, and she lived happily in the garden for many, many years.

Gold-Tree — Silver-Tree

Once there was a king who lived happily with his queen, Silver-Tree, and his beautiful daughter called Gold-Tree.

One day Silver-Tree and Gold-Tree were sitting by a pool and Silver-Tree decided to peer into the water and talk to the trout swimming there: "Silver trout in the pool, who is the most beautiful woman in the world?"

"Gold-Tree is the most beautiful," said the fish.

Silver-Tree was mad with jealousy. She could not stand the fact that someone could be beautiful than she, so she decided to get Gold-Tree killed, and to be sure the girl was dead, she would eat Gold-Tree's heart and liver. The queen was so mad with jealousy that she told her husband, begging him to kill their daughter.

At just this time it happened that a prince from a far country had come to ask for Gold-Tree's hand in marriage. The king, a good man, seeing that the two young people loved each other, took his chance and sent the two off to be married. Then, when out hunting, he took a deer's heart and liver, and gave them to his wife. Once she had eaten these, Silver-Tree was cured of her jealousy.

All was well until the queen again asked the fish who was the most beautiful, and he replied, "Gold-Tree, your daughter, is the fairest."

"My daughter is long dead!" exclaimed the queen.

"Surely she is not. For she has married a fine prince in a far country."

Her husband told her that this was true.

"Make ready the great ship, for I must visit my daughter," said Silver-Tree.

And because she had seemed cured of her jealousy, the king let her go.

The prince was out hunting when Silver-Tree arrived. Gold-Tree realised that her life was in danger, so she called her servants who locked her in her room.

But Silver-Tree was cunning. She called sweetly, "Put your little finger through the keyhole, so your mother may kiss it."

As soon as it appeared, the wicked queen took a dagger dipped in poison and stuck it into Gold-Tree's finger. Straight away, the princess collapsed and died, the dagger still in her finger.

When Gold-Tree's husband returned, he saw his young wife dead on the floor. She was so beautiful that he preserved her body locked in her room, and kept the key himself.

Some years later, the prince's grief faded a little, but he never smiled, and he decided to marry once again.

One day his second wife found the key to the dead girl's room. She was curious to see an unknown part of her husband's castle, so she quietly opened the door and went in. When she saw the beautiful body she realised at once that this must be Gold-Tree, for she had heard the tale of the girl's death. She saw the poisoned dagger still stuck in the girl's finger. Yes, this must be Gold-Tree.

Still curious, the second wife pulled at the dagger to remove it, and Gold-Tree rose, alive, just as she was before her mother's visit.

The second wife said to the prince, "What would you give me if I made you laugh again?"

"Nothing could make me laugh, unless Gold-Tree was alive again," said the prince sadly.

The wife took the prince to see Gold-Tree. A change came over her husband and the second wife knew that Gold-Tree was his true love, and that she must leave.

But the prince was so grateful to her that he would not let her go.

Everything went well for them living together in the palace until Silver-Tree talked to the fish again and discovered that Gold-Tree was still alive and was still the most beautiful woman in the world.

And so Silver-Tree went to visit her daughter, and again the prince was out when she arrived. Gold-Tree quaked with fear when she saw her mother approaching.

"Let us go to meet her," said the second wife calmly.

Silver-Tree held out a precious gold cup. "I bring a refreshing drink for my daughter," she said.

The second wife looked at her coldly. "It is our custom for the visitor to drink first," she said.

Silver-Tree raised the cup to her mouth, but she knew that if she drank, she would kill herself. Just at that moment, the second wife struck the cup, sending some of the deadly poison straight down Silver-Tree's throat. The wicked queen fell dead to the floor. At last, Gold-Tree, the prince, and his second wife could live in peace.

Sleeping Beauty

Once upon a time, in a land far, far away, there lived a king and queen who were kind and good. When the queen gave birth to a baby girl, the whole kingdom rejoiced.

When it was time for the baby to be christened, the king

and queen arranged a great celebration. They asked the seven good fairies of the kingdom to be the baby's godmothers. But eight fairies arrived at the feast.

The eighth fairy was ugly and old, and no one had seen her for years. The king and queen, thinking she was dead, hadn't invited her to take part in the ceremony.

Soon it was time for the fairies to give the baby princess their magical presents. The first gave her the gift of beauty, the second gave her wisdom. The third fairy said she would be graceful, the fourth said that she would dance like the wind. The fifth and sixth gave her the gift of music and song, so that she would sing and play like an angel.

Just before the seventh fairy stepped up to give the princess her gift, the eighth fairy pushed in front of her.

"On her sixteenth birthday, the princess," she cackled, "will prick her finger on the spindle of a spinning wheel – and she will die!"

Everyone in the room was horrified, and the queen began to cry.

But then the seventh fairy stepped forward. "Here is my gift," she said. "The princess will not die. Instead, when she pricks her finger, she will fall asleep for a hundred years. At the end of that time, a prince will come to wake her up."

The king and queen were relieved, but even so they ordered every spinning wheel in the kingdom to be destroyed. They couldn't bear to think of anything hurting their daughter.

The years passed and the princess grew into a lovely young girl, as wise, beautiful and graceful as the fairies had promised.

On the day of her sixteenth birthday, she was wandering through the castle when she came to a small room in a tall tower. Inside, an old woman sat spinning thread.

"My dear," cackled the old woman, "come here and try this for yourself."

As soon as the princess's hand touched the spindle, she pricked her finger and fell to the floor in a deep sleep.

When they discovered their daughter, the king and queen were heartbroken, for they knew that she would not wake for a hundred years. They called for the palace guard, who gently laid the sleeping princess on a golden stretcher and carried her to the royal bedchamber. There they placed her on a bed with silken pillows and velvet covers. The king and queen watched over her and cried.

"Oh, my dear," said the queen to her husband. "How are we ever going to cope without our darling daughter?"

The fairy who had saved the princess's life heard what had happened. Worried that the princess would wake up in a world where she knew no one, she cast a spell over the whole castle. Everyone, from the guards and the kitchen maids to the gardeners and the cooks – even the princess's pet dog – fell into a deep, deep sleep.

Then the fairy made tall trees and twisting, sharp brambles grow around the castle, surrounding it with a thick thorny wall that no one could get through. Only the very tops of the castle's towers could be seen.

And so a hundred years went by.

One day, a prince from a nearby land was out riding when he saw the tops of the castle towers rising from the middle of the thick, dark wood. He asked some of the country people about the castle, and they told him the story of the Sleeping Beauty.

"Many people have wanted to get through those thorns," they told him, "but they have all died trying."

The prince was determined to be the one who succeeded and set off towards the mysterious castle.

To the prince's amazement, the thorny brambles and the twisting branches of the dark trees let him pass through easily. He reached the castle door, and went inside.

The prince walked through many halls and chambers where people and animals slept as if they were dead. He searched every room and chamber, until he found the very one where the beautiful princess slept.

"Oh, princess!" cried the prince. "You are more beautiful than the most delicate rose ever found."

The prince moved quietly towards the sleeping princess and gazed down lovingly at her. He gently took her tiny hand in his, and as love filled his heart, he knelt beside her and slowly kissed her red lips. Instantly the princess's eyes opened.

"Is it you, my prince?" she said, when she saw him. "I have waited such a long time for you!"

At that moment the spell was broken, and everyone else in the castle woke up, too.

That evening, the princess's sixteenth birthday was celebrated with a joyous party – a hundred years too late!

The princess and her prince danced together all evening, and soon after, were married. They lived together in happiness for many, many years.